THE MISSING

Juliet Bates

I0741794

The Linen Press

'This is the kind of novel I love. The writing is exquisite and conveys the dream-like sense of 'lost' people wandering Europe with sad tales to tell which may or may not be true... a brilliant novel.'

— Sally Zigmond, *The Elephant in the Writing Room*

'A deliciously descriptive book that questions the notion of memories and the idea of believing what you want to believe.'

— Secluded Charm

'Totally absorbing... a beautifully written and constructed book.'

— Alison Bacon, *Between the Lines*

Published in the UK by
The Linen Press
75c(13) South Oswald Rd
EDINBURGH
EH9 2HH
www.linenpressbooks.co.uk

First published by The Linen Press, April 2009

ISBN 978-0-9559618-2-3

Typeset and designed by Initial Typesetting Services, Edinburgh

CONTENTS

PREFACE

There was a time when they were always finding Anastasias, fishing them out of the sea like mermaids or stumbling over them in mad houses and hospitals. The girls kept coming in waves from the east, one after another, beached on the right side of the border, their memories washed out. Each one said that she was the real Grand Duchess, escaped from the bullets and the bayonets, and each one had those gently slanting eyes and that red blonde hair. They would sit blank faced in hospital beds or apartment rooms with river mud still in the folds of their ears or sand in the creases of their toes, waiting for grainy photographs to be taken and comparisons to be made. Speaking in half sentences, confusing the sounds of Russian, English and German, they would talk of childhoods spent inside a jewel box palace, or of happy Easters with gifts of golden eggs. They would remember the panelled carriages of the Imperial train, the silver samovars, the braided soldiers, the cream canvas sails of the Black Sea yacht. Then the girls would weep and, pointing to the scars on their necks and their hands, each one would swear, over and over, that she was the real princess, the real Anastasia, as if the repetition made it true.

Quietly, in the evenings when the light was faint, they might recite the names of the imprisoned family – Mama, Papa, Olga and Tatiana, Maria, Anastasia, Alexis. The girls' cracked lips and dry tongues would whisper the list like a litany. They said that the family had waited, counting the long days, listening to rumours and mutterings beyond the walls. Hope swung back and forth like a pendulum, but no one came. The father and his daughters paced the muddy grounds, while the jailers watched – stone headed soldiers or gentle boys with faces soft as summer plums. And upstairs the mother prayed beside her son with the bleeding bruises.

Sometimes – but only ever in the dark – the girls might remember other things. Then they would struggle with the words, short gasps escaping between each phrase:

'A July night. . . a basement. . . vaulted ceiling. . . striped wallpaper. . . wooden boards.'

In this room the family waited again, the boy seated next to his parents, his sisters standing behind clutching pillows packed with diamonds, feeling rubies and sapphires sharp against their ribs. They waited, and the hands of the father's watch ticked on, and the mother knotted her fingers together in prayer, and the boy's dog whimpered gently.

Then someone shouted, and the soldiers raised their rifles. They fired bullets into soft flesh, beat butts against bone, slashed skin with bayonets. The corsets of the sisters spewed precious stones and the falling bodies spewed blood. The gunshots pierced cloth, plaster and the floor where the dead lay. Then the blood gushed, running into gaps, crevices and spirals in the wood grain. It soaked right down into the boards.

The stories were always the same until the shooting, then they parted like a cross roads, wandering and twisting in new directions. The first Anastasia said she had been rescued by a soldier. They had made their way through the battlefields, tripping over the bodies of white guards and red guards as they went. The second girl had pushed her way out of the house, and had run through the bullets to the forest. Then, hiding in the bracken, she had eaten berries when she could find them, and dry leaves when she couldn't. The third Anastasia had been saved by her father's servants. They had wrapped her in furs, concealed her in the back of a wagon and slowly dragged her westwards towards the border.

When their stories were over the girls would cry a little. Then dabbing their eyes, they would ask to see their family – a royal aunt or an imperial grandmother: but the relatives never came.

For a while those poor flimsy shadows were pushed and pulled and measured and judged by exiled colonels or journalists who wished to make a little money. The girls were tested in palace protocol and family lore. They were examined from head to damaged foot. Each tiny birthmark, each beauty spot was mapped like a landmark in black-backed notebooks. The girls' posture and comportment were scrutinised by minor princes, and their shaky writing inspected by experts, but there was always something that didn't fit: a word or a gesture, the tone of their voice, the arch of an eyebrow. They were simply not convincing, and fake Anastasias no longer made the headlines of newspapers or women's magazines.

The months passed. No one came to the hospitals or the apartments any more. The girls waited, expecting questions, but no one came. It was said that they were fortune hunters. It was said that they were liars or mad women with a fixation on a missing Grand Duchess whose body lay, no doubt, with the rest of her family, half burnt, down a mine shaft in a forest clearing.

The Anastasias grew up, and some gave up, disappeared, melting back into the city or the sea again. Others moved abroad to countries where there was thick snow and birch trees. They lived on farms or in rotting bungalows with too many dogs, and continued to greet people in their childhood language, holding out the back of a hand like a princess. Even in their new homes they rehearsed the myths, adding details here and there: the exchange of a diamond for a rotten cabbage, a handful of pearls for a bowl of soup. And as they aged, nothing changed. Each woman was still her Imperial Highness the Grand Duchess Anastasia, the youngest daughter of the last Tsar.

PART 1

At the top of the house, under the eaves, is the basket containing the clothes. The girl pulls out the velvet, the silk and the linen. She hopes that the cloak she wraps around her shoulders and the hat she places on her head will allow her to change or to disappear.

HARBIN'S STORY

It was Lloyd Harbin who told me about them at a party over by the park. At first I didn't want to hear. I was thinking of leaving, I remember. My head pounded and the tight armholes of my dress had begun to rub. It was one of those shrill, bright nights, full of laughter and champagne. I tried to laugh too and I drank too much, but it didn't change my mood. Halfway through the evening I watched my reflection in the large mirror that hung over the mantelpiece. I smiled like everyone else, held my glass high, but amongst all the colour – the brunettes and the blondes – I looked grey and mouse small, drenched in dust and book spores from the dim-lit hush of the reading rooms where I had sat all afternoon.

I was searching for my wrap in the guest room when Harbin came waddling up to me waving a mushroom vol-au-vent in one fat hand and a glass of champagne in the other.

'Got something for you, Fran,' he said. 'A story, a princess story,' and he took me by the arm and led me out onto the balcony. It was a May midnight and still warm. I could feel the heat of the traffic, and I could see drops of perspiration on Harbin's puffy face sparkling like glass in the moonlight.

He told me that he was acting as a legal advisor to one of the Anastasias.

'A mean-faced crazy woman. Still trying to prove who she isn't.' He wiped the sweat from his face with his shirt sleeve.

3

Harbin said that she had been found by an exiled gardener who had tended the roses in the grounds of the palace before the revolution. The man was fishing for trout when he saw a girl wading out against the current into the middle of the estuary. For some time she stood looking towards the sea. Then the sun caught her face, and the gardener noticed the way that she held her head, the slope of her shoulders, and the colour of her hair. He saw the flecks of blue in her eyes, the pink of her lips. He watched the water dripping from her eyelashes and rolling down her cheeks, and he saw the white petticoat clinging to her scarred skin. Believing suddenly in miracles, in resurrections, he ran towards her, shouting her name. Then he took her home, dried her clothes, and cooked the muddy fish from the river. He called the girl Malenkaya.

'She became quite a celebrity,' said Harbin, 'always signing autographs and dancing with princes. Then one night she forgot herself, made a slip. She was dropped and they found someone else to take her place.'

He laughed gently.

'She still thinks she can fool them, says there's a stash of Imperial money somewhere, or jewels, or a great big Fabergé egg hidden in a London bank vault. Christ, is she crazy. Make a great story, though.'

Little fragments of pastry from the vol-au-vent drifted like gold leaf into his champagne glass. They bobbed for a while on the bubbles and then dropped slowly to the bottom.

I must have smiled at him and said something noncommittal like, 'She sounds interesting, Lloyd,' but in truth there were fabulous qualities to Harbin's tale that irritated me. The story was forty years old and it hardly seemed worth reviving. After the hard, quick-witted brightness of that night, I wanted to write about sharp things, solid and contemporary. I was tired of old stories, tired of research. The endless forages through newspapers and rotting books frustrated me, and I had become unhappy in the library basement where the arched windows were barred against the light, where every movement, every turning of the page was magnified threefold by the echoing spaces.

That was how I had spent the afternoon before the party, stumbling over syllables, and reading and rereading the few phrases I had written until they lost all sense. The dull words I had chosen during the day seemed to hang around me and weigh me down that evening as I tried to match the sharp talk. My voice sounded flat, I spoke too slowly and the things I said were leaden and plodding. I wanted to leave and was irritated that Lloyd Harbin had managed to trap me on the balcony. He grasped my bare arm and I could feel his warm damp breath on my face as he spoke, but I did not want to meet his Duchess, nor write about her story. I simply smiled and nodded at him. Then with the vague promise of a lunch date, I finally succeeded in slipping past Harbin's bulk, and left him on the balcony, contentedly sipping his champagne and listening to the cars driving down the avenue.

For several weeks after the party, I managed to elude Lloyd Harbin Believing that his story was merely a pretext for seeing me again, I resolved not to answer my doorbell, and I avoided restaurants that he frequented. I even decided to remain in my apartment until I was certain that he was safely inside his office. In those days I lived on the edge of Greenwich Village not far from Harbin's home, and I had often seen him lumbering along the streets in the morning and the early evening. Gradually, however, as the weather grew hotter and as the bitter memories of the party began to fade. I dismissed Lloyd Harbin and his Duchess from my mind. I had other things to trouble me then.

At the beginning of June my father became quite ill. He lived alone, some distance from the city, and I was obliged to stay with him while I made arrangements for his care. Strangely, during those days that we spent together, my normally tight-lipped father grew quite loquacious. After a lifetime of silence, it seemed that he needed to fill his last few months with conversation.

The Missing

We had always been remote and uncommunicative. For many years we had avoided each other completely. I remember that even as a child I would deliberately wait until he had left a room and wandered away before I would enter it. We could pass entire weeks like that, not talking to one another at all apart from the necessary discussions concerning meals and school. The silence became a habit that was easier to maintain than to break. It seemed more dignified to remain taciturn and it removed the need to talk of feelings and hopes.

As I grew older, we managed to sustain a relationship of sorts comfortably distanced from one another; a relationship based on one short telephone call each month when my father would report on his health and I would talk about something bland like the films I had seen or the books I had read. He never asked me about my writing.

We continued those reserved, polite exchanges until his illness, until his last year. Only then did we really begin to talk to one another, although intermittently and, in my case, often angrily, because what he said pulled me backwards. After each conversation, I found myself scrabbling around in the dark trying to remember, trying to piece the fragments together again.

My father had always lived in the same house, a long white building balanced on a hill above a tidal creek that eventually ran into the sea. His house marked the end of an impasse. The road that led to the garden finished there, in the grass. It was perhaps for this reason that he had few visitors, only those who really wished to see him.

The house and the church were separated from the town of Bluewood by a forest. In the winter, the mist and chimney smoke hung about the trees making the pine fronds change from black-green to a sort of chalky grey, and in the spring, bluebells grew beneath the trees. As a child I was not allowed to play there, and as a consequence the forest became imbued with a dreadful mystery that seemed to drape over the trees like a cloak as soon as the sun disappeared. I never liked to stay out too long for fear that something might come blundering out of those trees and grab me.

I played in the garden, picked the flowers or sat on the swing whose ropes were wound round the branch of an apple tree. Sometimes I used to run my hand along the wall that sheltered the plums and the blueberry bushes, looking for dips and holes in which treasure might be hidden. I had always hoped I might discover a gold coin or a diamond ring in those weathered niches, although the only objects I did find were rusting plaques screwed into the wall seventy years before to remind the gardener of the names of the fruit that had been planted there.

At the end of the drive was a rockery where short grey lavender and tumbling purple aubrietia grew. Once I found a nickel buried amongst the flowers and for several days afterwards I returned and pushed my fingers into the dense leaves, penetrating down to the dirt, hoping for more. I didn't find another coin and was scolded for flattening the plants and damaging the tiny flowers. The edges of my finger nails were ingrained with dusty soil for weeks afterwards.

It is the garden I remember, not the house. That was my father's domain. I was told to be silent as I climbed the stairs, instructed not to slam my feet flat on the bare boards above his study and asked not to shout too loudly or sing because he worked so hard. My father was a business man, a wealthy and successful one, and we had none of the worries about money that I have now. I don't suppose he ever knew or could even imagine the frustration that poverty brings: the high walled limitations, the dreariness at the end of the month, or the heart-beating fear of spending too much. In many ways I was probably a spoilt child. If I asked politely for something I always received it, and I was well educated and well travelled. Every year my father insisted on taking me somewhere and showing me something – a city, a famous building or a battlefield.

But I think the best time, in fact the only time I remember really being with him, was on the water. Sometimes in the spring and summer we took the canoe and paddled down the creek to the junction where it joined the river. I liked that feeling of moving low through the water and trailing my hand in the river's coldness. When I was older, I would kneel at the front of the boat and paddle inefficiently, for it was my father who both directed and powered the canoe. Sometimes we would pull into a bank and sit by the honeysuckle bushes where I would examine the flowers that grew there. Then, in mid summer we would take sandwiches and coffee and explore the flat sand islands that lay in the middle of the river. While my father photographed the water, I scanned the horizon from those islands, identifying our house and the skyline of the town on the opposite bank. I could sit for hours charting the once familiar buildings that had been twisted and turned into something strange by my new outlook. It was like seeing a place for the first time.

When I arrived at Bluewood during the late stages of my father's illness, I noticed that the canoe, which had always been kept on the banks of the creek, had been pulled up onto the gravel outside the house. It was lying on its side by the back door like the carcass of a large dead fish. It clearly hadn't been used for several years because the wood was dull grey and soft in places, and the name, which he had painted along the edge, *Natty*, had vanished completely. Later, sitting in his study, I asked him about the canoe, and he told me haltingly that he had stopped using it three years ago following a particularly upsetting incident.

He had set out one morning, paddling only occasionally, letting the boat gently drift with the tide. For a while, he sat looking at the ochre islands in the distance and at the birds on the sand banks. Then he had lowered his eyes and rested them on the water. Watching the ripples form and disappear, he noticed something else floating towards him, a form shrouded in green cloth, the size of a corpse. It was swollen and knotted with seaweed. My father stared at it, horrified, as it came alongside the canoe. For a second he considered turning round, and paddling away, but the appalling shape refused to be ignored and butted sickeningly and softly against the side of the canoe. He gripped the paddle and frantically stabbed at the object with the wooden blade. The form bobbed up and down on the surface of the water and then the cloth began to unravel. He held his breath and looked down, but there was nothing inside. It was just a large piece of green sacking which unrolled into a flat length and floated away like a bad joke. He never took the canoe out again.

After recounting this story, he sighed deeply. Then slowly, he began to talk again, working steadily backwards, recalling small events that I had long forgotten. It was as if the story of the canoe had evoked other stories, memories of his past and my childhood. He spoke about the trip we made to Europe when I was fifteen, and of the birthday picnics by the river. He talked about my mother, about their wedding and their long honeymoon. Then he paused and reached over to take my hand. We rarely touched, and I was both surprised and embarrassed by this sudden display of affection.

'Do you remember the cemetery?' he asked. 'Père-Lachaise. Do you remember it?'

I had never been there and I waited for him to explain, but his thoughts seemed to weave together and grow confused.

'She wore a yellow butterfly dress,' he said. 'She had sloping shoulders and white hands. And there was a cat, I think.'

'I don't understand,' I said quietly.

He looked up at me and his eyes, which until then had been unfocused and damp, became sharper. He began again, and as I listened to his thin voice, I shivered despite the warmth of the room. Removing my hand from his, I slid it into my jacket pocket to stop the tips of my fingers numbing.

The Missing

My father talked for two hours that afternoon. He didn't tell me everything, only presented me with vague outlines that he would later flesh out and describe in more detailed episodes all through the summer. When he had finished he stretched over and kissed me on the cheek. I think he was relieved that I had taken it so well.

At the end of the week I escorted my father to the nursing home. He seemed resigned about leaving the white house. He didn't even turn his head to look at the garden or the creek one last time before the taxi drove away down the lane. When we arrived at the home however, he had to be helped out of the car by two nurses and, as he leaned against them, I noticed that he was shaking. It was as if the sight of their uniforms had reminded him suddenly that he would never see his home again.

That evening I took the train back to the city and for the first time in several days I was able to contemplate the things he had told me. I repeated his words in my head while I pictured the cemetery and the woman in her butterfly dress. I saw the slope of her shoulders and her white freckled hands as she drifted past me and climbed the stone steps, but when she reached the point where the paths divided, she faded, then disappeared. However hard I tried, I could not recall her image again for each time she was supplanted by someone else: a girl with water streaming over her hair and face.

Slowly I realised who she was and the memory of that shiny May midnight party rose in my mind again. As I remembered how Lloyd Harbin had described his Anastasia my objections to working on his story began to subside. Perhaps it was the small coincidences that forced me to draw parallels between my father's memories and Harbin's tale. Or maybe the Duchess was merely an excuse and I was trying to blot out what my father had told me.

LILA, PAULA AND THE DUCHESS

I was always looking for stories. At that time I wrote for a magazine called *Twenty-Eight,* predictably named because it was published on the twenty-eighth day of every month. It had a certain reputation. Hemingway and Scott Fitzgerald had written for it in the thirties, and after the war it was still considered weighty and significant. It was a magazine run by clever men who wrote with a punch like a blow from a tight knuckled fist, men who knew about the intricacies of baseball and who drank with the artists down at the Cedar Tavern. In those days, I would open the front cover and instead of the printing ink, I smelt the odour of masculine ambition, sweat, and the sea shore.

My articles were pushed towards the end of the magazine, lodged between the theatre and restaurant listings. Every month I seemed to slide further and further towards the back cover, until I thought that one day I might fall out of the magazine altogether. I couldn't write the hard-boiled, clever prose that was fashionable. My writing was too lyrical and singsong. It had a touch of the other world. I wrote small stories about the strange, the missing, the reinvented. I wrote about an illusionist famous for making clouds of pink winged moths appear and disappear by a simple click of her fingers, and a radio star with a made-up past. I wrote about ghosts and phantom voices, and that terrible tornado in the twenties when the sky grew black with things: clothes, cars, babies and cows somersaulting in the air. I did have a few successes. There was praise from other writers and the promise of a book, but nothing ever emerged, and after several years, those little hopes that had been nourished rapidly faded like weak sunlight in winter.

I continued to compose the stories for *Twenty-Eight*, but gradually I found that I was unable to arrange the phrases properly on the page, or put them in the right order. I would spend hours shuffling through the dictionary for the meanings of the words that I used, doubting everything I wrote. Then I discovered that I could no longer read the notes that I had taken, and even my typescripts seemed faint and smudged. I started to wear glasses, blaming my poor sight on the books I had been consulting, and the shadows under which I had been sitting, but they didn't seem to help. I remained at my desk day after day, thinking only of the food I might cook that evening, or the clothes I might wear the next morning. They were small propulsions forward, a way of imagining a future. I would attend to each thing at a certain moment and at the same time every day. It was a clockwork life characterised by dressing, lunching, going to the library or trying to write my notes.

It is odd therefore that, on the evening of my return from the nursing home, the words came so easily. As soon as I entered my apartment I sat down at my desk and noted everything that I could remember of Lloyd Harbin's tale. The following morning I rang Harbin, and we ate together in a small French restaurant off Madison avenue. At first he seemed surprised at my renewed interest in the Duchess, and slightly reluctant that I should pursue the story. Then, as he realised that I was more persistent than he had at first thought, Harbin told me about the other Anastasias. There were two more, he said. He had corresponded with them both whilst he had been researching the Duchess's claims.

'I'm warning you, Fran,' Harbin leaned towards me over the table. 'They're all as crazy as each other.'

Lila, Paula and the Duchess

That afternoon I went to the library and, as I began to read, I discovered that it was their lies that fascinated me, their confusion between the real and the unreal, and the mess of stories that formed their imagined past. I wanted to know what they had become and what they had left behind: name, family, language, even perhaps their memory. I was waiting for their mistakes that would tell me who they were really were.

The three Anastasias lived out of the city in places with names as hopeful as Bountiful and Sunnyside and as sorry as Pityme. All the towns were the same, however: a main street and short tributaries that ran off into the countryside, ending at a forest or a ploughed field or a dried out prairie where the soil was powder grey. Everything was grey. I looked out of the train window at the shades of slate and steel on the hills, at the bone silver trees that grew by the edge of the railroad. It was as if the sun had soaked up the brightness, blotted out the colour, and the heat haze had dropped down in front of the landscape like a monochrome veil.

The first Anastasia lived by the sea. She owned a small wooden cabin and a grubby yard, edged by a barrier of criss-cross wire that had been buckled and distorted by the weight of an ancient hound. When I arrived, the dog lay across the gateway like the guardian of hell, keeping the dead inside and the living out. It was damp in the yard despite the aridness of that June. The dirt of the empty flower beds was moist, there were fermenting pools of spring rainwater in the dips and cracks of the concrete, and in the back yard, where the sun could not reach was a bed frame whitened by lichen and age. Yet, when Lila opened the door to greet me, I could see that the interior of the cabin was like a fairy castle, a palace filled with gilded objects: chipped statuettes splashed with gold paint, heavy framed prints of doll eyed children, and Swiss chalet music boxes, homes to figurines that danced to a wind-up tune.

Lila was a pastel woman, dressed in dulled eau de nil and dove blue. She was mild enough, a little mad perhaps. She answered my questions obliquely, responding in broken phrases or in single words, as if she knew that grammar and coherent sentences would damage her claims. Her tale was confused and muddled. For Lila, it seemed, there was no past, present or future. Time had not progressed, rather it had lurched backwards and forwards, folding and merging so much that she couldn't unpick it.

About the escape from the Siberian house she could tell me very little, nor could she recall who had helped or how she had made her way onto the sinking ship. She just shook her head and mumbled into the tea cup that she held in her hand:

'No remember.'

I was patient, and after several hours of gentle questioning, she began to recount how she had found herself again. Then haltingly, as if she were searching for the best words, she described the moment when she had discovered who she really was.

Lying face down in a shallow sea, looking at the shells and the sand, Lila had seen pearls and gold dust. Someone had dragged her out, placing their hands under her arms and pulling her onto the beach. There were others, she said, who were lying there too, drying in the breeze, watching the wrecked boat sink into the horizon. She lay looking upwards at the faces in the clouds, trying to put names to them, but they floated away too quickly for her to recognise their features.

Later, a man helped her up and she was taken to a house on a cliff that overlooked the sea, a summer house with a pillared entrance. It was empty, she said, and seemed to be a ghost house for there were white cloths draped over the chairs and the tables. She was made to sit down, given water and tea and a little brandy. People moved around her, came and went, swayed in front of her.

She looked around the room, at the silk carpet on the floor, at the pictures on the walls, and she saw curves. It was the curves that helped her to remember. The blue knotted tendrils woven into the carpet were the same as those in the rugs and runners that lay over the floors of the palace. The carved arabesques in the picture frames were like those that had surrounded the photographs propped on the desk in her father's study. Then suddenly the whole world was full of curves, arcs, eddies and whirlpools that tied her up, paralysed her and pulled her down.

She must have collapsed, she said, and when she recovered she remembered who she really was.

They were kind to her at first. They took her to a large apartment in a city where there was a nurse to care for her and a gentleman to visit her every day. She could not remember the gentleman's name, but he had a beard, she said, a pointed beard, and a diamond-headed tie pin that glinted bright like an owl's eye when he talked. He asked her questions in words that she could not understand. It was as if she were still under the sea and could hear his voice above her. The sounds were familiar, but were muffled by the noise of the waves that washed over her. Sometimes other people came to the apartment, although they moved too quickly and she could not see their faces. When she was alone, the room was black and still. She could see a pin-hole light in the distance like a tunnel exit, but it was so far away she knew she could never reach it.

Then one day in spring, the nurse handed her a bag containing a set of clothes: a skirt and jacket made from rough wool, and a white blouse that had been sewn so hurriedly that the cotton threads still hung from it. She gave the girl a passport, a purse containing a small amount of money and a train ticket. Then she led her to the door and gently pushed her out into the street. Blindly, Lila found her way to a station, then fumbled her way onto a train, then a ship, then another train, until finally she found herself in the small grey hut by the sea.

Two weeks later I travelled to the home of the second Anastasia. By then the heat haze had disappeared and had been replaced by a thin curtain of drizzle, but still the landscape was grey, a flat northern grey of treeless high lands that seemed to stretch for years. From the road I could see Paula's farm, a collection of wooden framed buildings covered in ancient shingles. I had hired a cab, and the driver, who didn't want to muddy his car, insisted on waiting for me by the farm gate. So I walked to the house along a track covered in decomposing leaves and fragments of feed sacks. On both sides of the lane lay the remains of derelict tractors or wagons, and in the fields were shards of corrugated metal that had blown off the roofs of old barns and had stuck like daggers in the ground. The yard was empty apart from some chickens pecking the mud and two crusted milk churns posted outside the back door like sentries. I waited a while, then I saw her walking from one shed to another, bucket in hand. She seemed taller than she should have been, taller than the real princess. She wore rubber boots and waxed clothes, and the water ran off her. She said later that she didn't like the rain to touch her.

I had written several letters to Paula asking her to see me. A week before my visit to the farm she had finally agreed, but as I greeted her on that dirty afternoon she seemed doubtful once more.

'What I tell you is private,' she said, pulling off her boots in the porch.

She wasn't fickle or capricious; she was just worried that, in telling her story, the sorry episodes in her life might repeat themselves. We sat at her kitchen table and I tried to reassure her, explaining about the magazine, and my interest in her story. She looked at me hopefully like a timid hungry dog, then agreed that I could print the interview, saying sorrowfully,

'What I tell you is finished, over. After this I don't want to think about it any more.'

Her story was short. She told it as quickly as she could sitting in the dark of her kitchen, the hood of her coat still pulled up over her head. They had found her, she said, sleeping in a storm, like a drenched

16

cat in a doorway. She was pregnant, carrying a dead child inside her belly. She had always known who she was, hers was not a case of lost memory or confusion. She told them her name straight away, but from that moment onwards, her life was hell because no one believed her. She was taunted and mocked, moved from hospital to asylum, but the more she protested, the smaller the cell, the tighter the straitjacket, the stronger the pill. When she ceased to insist on her story they let her go, and she wandered aimlessly west until she met a man who brought her to the farm. They married, and she changed her name to Paula. It seemed easier to change both names at once, to be someone new, she said.

There was no mystery in her story, only sadness. I think she must have drowned her misery in pig muck and chicken feed.

My journey to the home of the third Anastasia was complicated by a late train, and it was a long, lonely trip. To me there is nothing more alienating than travelling in the dark of an empty train watching the shadows on the horizon, the silhouettes of barns, houses or trees. They are desolate places beside the railway tracks, sad dreary smears on the landscape. I looked out imagining what it would be like to live there, or there, or there: a monotonous life regulated by passing trains marking the movement of time. After a while I pulled the blind down and tried to read my notes, but the light was so feeble over my head that I closed my eyes instead. I saw Paula's face again half hidden by the hood: a narrow slit of forehead, a protruding nose, the centre of her closed mouth, and the water that continued to slip down over her hood and onto her shoulders like tears.

By the time the train had reached its destination I had grown accustomed to the quiet grey dusk. This new station was a surprise of announcements and light, and there were crowds of people walking towards me or crossing my path. I pushed against them, arriving at the exit where I joined a line of passengers waiting for taxis. Standing with my back to the town, looking inwards to the station, I noticed a young man who was waiting for someone. He was like a sparrow, all fragile bones and nervousness, twisting and turning, peering out at the taxi line, or in at the trains. Strangely, in that flat, bright, light he seemed familiar to me. It must have been the way he held his head to one side, or the way his arms hung from his slightly drooping shoulders, that reminded me of myself in photographs which were taken when I was fifteen or sixteen years old. I wondered whether I should go to him, imagining for a moment that it was for me that he was waiting, but after a few minutes, he was greeted by an older man who had come from a far-off platform. I watched them as they walked away together out of the station. The man seemed sure of himself, he strode confidently along, but beside him the boy hesitated, hunching his shoulders and sliding his hands into the pockets of his coat.

I stayed in the town for one restless night and in the morning I took another train to the home of the third Anastasia, Lloyd Harbin's Duchess. Harbin had already told me that she was the only pretender to be taken seriously by the exiled Imperial family and its hangers on. She certainly possessed enough regality in her cheek bones and in her posture to suggest a royal background. She also knew how to deal with those almost imperceptible things that make so much difference: how to wear clothes, how to stand, how to address others. If she wasn't Anastasia – and I am sure she was not – she must have received an aristocratic education in some lost castle in the depths of the Urals, or a Crimean Palace, long before the revolution.

Despite its dismal exterior the Duchess's apartment was a pleasure, open and bright. It seemed to be infused with a nordic light, the sort of hazy brilliance associated with reflected snow and ice. There was a chain of rooms, a reception room leading to a dining room leading, I suppose, to a bedroom. The floors were polished parquet, the walls were panelled, the plaster tinted a pale blue and the woodwork white. The furniture was not fake palatial as in Lila's hut, but was made up of rather austere, solitary pieces: a desk, a side table, and a set of upright chairs. It had all been pushed back against the walls as if a dance or some sort of state function were about to take place.

The Duchess arrived from the end room trailing chiffon and lace. She was too old, I thought. Her hands trembled, she stooped, and despite the makeup that she had smoothed over the lines and pouches of her face she looked at least ten or fifteen years older than the real Anastasia would have been. Midway across the room, as if she had guessed my thoughts, she seemed to check herself. Twitching a girlish smile at me, she held out her hand, the tips of which she permitted me to touch in a sort of handshake. Then she asked had I read her memoirs. I had. Harbin had lent me a copy. I had thought the book dull: a list of elaborate names that I could not retain, and histories so confused and remote that I had found them difficult to follow. There were no intimate details in her writing, nothing to suggest an inside knowledge, only a brief description of the imprisonment and the shooting, followed by a bald explanation of her escape.

The Duchess claimed that she had been helped by servants who had hidden her in the back of a cart cushioned with furs. She felt safe with them and relied on their help. They dressed her wounds and bathed her face, and at night she slept well, forgetting the dreams that plagued her during the day. But one morning she awoke to find that she was alone in the cart. There were feathers and threads lying on the grass, and the horse was gone. The servants had ripped open the cushions into which she had sewn her jewels, and they had taken the food, the furs, and the grey pony that had pulled her across the border.

It had taken her a whole day to walk to the town, she said. When it grew dark she slept in the street, sitting upright on a step, leaning her head against a door frame. She spent several hungry days and nights there, worrying that someone might notice her and take her to the police. She soon moved on, wandering from town to town and village to village, working in a draper's shop, a bakery, and as a maidservant to a farmer's wife. Then finally she took a job in a workshop beside a large river, where she fashioned gloves for ladies. She was good at sewing the tiny stitches around the fine leather outlines of the hands and for two years she bent over a table making fingers and thumbs in canary yellow and powder blue kid.

In the summer, after the girls had put away the leather, thread and needles, and had taken off their aprons, they would bathe in the river. On one such evening, after the Duchess had been paddling near a stone bridge, she stood on the bank drying her hair. As she combed her fingers through the damp strands, a band of sunlight lit up her face. From the bridge she heard a man cry out, then he ran towards her, down the stone steps to the river bank. Kneeling in the mud he kissed the damp edge of her shift and called her by her real name.

The Duchess told me this almost word for word as it was printed in her book. She added tension by widening her eyes, or raising her hands, and she injected an air of melancholy through brief silences and moments of calm. She said that the family had accepted her, that a reunion of sorts had taken place, that they had given her dresses and lent her jewels. But it didn't last, she said. Someone started a rumour, and then the rumour spread, and like a virus, it destroyed her story until there was nothing left.

'The rumours were lies,' she said. 'All lies. They wouldn't listen to me any more. I wrote letters, but they sent them back unopened.'

She paused. Then she dropped her hands into her lap and lowered her head. She was like an actress at the end of a tragic scene who waits for the lights to fade and the curtain to fall.

'So sad, so sad,' she whispered.

As if to change the mood, she asked the maid to make some tea. It arrived in a Wedgwood pot accompanied by matching cups, and a cake stand piled with stale biscuits. She sipped her tea delicately and began to talk about her life in the town, the dreariness of the days, the anxious nights. Then she told me about her dreams, vivid ones, more real than life, she said. They had disturbed her sleep for years.

She would be running through a strange landscape – a thick forest or a mountain track – when, at the end of a path, she would come to a small hut. She would go inside, to find herself surrounded by clothes, books and photographs spread over the wooden floor. Gathering these things together, she would try to pack them quickly into a square-shaped suitcase that lay open in front of her, but the suitcase was always either too small for everything, or too heavy to carry, and she would have to leave something behind. Just as she was trying to decide, someone would come into the hut behind her, and then she would wake with her heart thudding.

'And there is one more,' she said. 'I go barefoot. I search for my shoes in the rooms of a large house, and when I find them, they are too small for my feet. I push and push but I can never squeeze them into the shape; I can never make them fit.'

After the interviews, the first few sentences of my article came easily enough. I looked at the page and I was pleased with what I had typed. As the days followed, however, the words began to slip from me again and I struggled to put the phrases together. Instead, I looked over at the photographs that lay beside my typewriter: little fat Lila posing next to a plaster saint, hooded Paula, and the Duchess in her royal suite. There were old photographs too, of the girls lying weary against hospital pillows and embroidered cushions, and there were poignant images of the Grand Duchess staring at the camera with a smile on her face. It was quite clear to me then that the three women were either liars or confused. There was no similarity, no chink of resemblance in their faces, in the way they sat or held their hands, or in the manner in which they winced tentative smiles at my camera lens. The poor girl was dead and had been for forty years, her body slowly rotting like the bed frame in Lila's back yard.

I doodled on the notepad beside my typewriter and wondered why such ornate lies had been imagined by ex-factory workers and refugee aristocrats: the erasing of one life and the replacement of it by something completely fictional. I had no answers and the patterns that I drew with my pen became deep troughs on the paper, grooves that I followed over and over again.

The article was published in September. It appeared for a few weeks on the pages of *Twenty-Eight* then disappeared again like the Anastasias themselves. I had written something, sent it out into a void where it floated for a short time until it was piled with other journals and newspapers under kitchen sinks, or tied in bundles and sent back to the publishers for shredding. Perhaps the story reappeared briefly in a smudged and torn version lying on a table in a doctor's or dentist's waiting room, but it elicited no response.

PIVKIN

In the autumn of that year my father died, but I felt nothing at first.

I went to the nursing home and collected his things. Then I took a cab to his house at Bluewood, where I had decided to stay while I organised the funeral. I got out of the car and looked at the early frost that had glazed the puddles in the drive, and I realised that I felt no emotions at all. It was as if I had just been anaesthetised and the numbness had washed over my entire body.

And yet the following day I experienced something I had never felt before, or at least, not with such intensity. I was making a telephone call to the undertaker when suddenly I suffered an acute shortness of breath which compelled me to end the conversation abruptly and lie flat on the couch in the study. I stayed there for the rest of the day, pinned down by the sickness. I thought that I had caught influenza or acquired some sort of respiratory problem. I even began to wonder whether I had developed asthma. Later, however, I decided that it was none of these.

As I sat in bed that evening, I began to understand that I was simply grappling with the impossible: the mystery of my father's absence. On the last day I had seen him alive, he had been sitting by the fireplace in the nursing home, clutching the blanket that covered his legs. But after his death three days later, when I returned to the home, I saw only his empty wheelchair and the folded blanket, and I knew that I would never hear his voice again.

The Missing

Once the funeral was over, I gave the rotting canoe to a neighbour's son, and I sold my father's car. I emptied the house, throwing years of journals and neatly stacked newspapers into the dustbin, folding his shirts and sweaters, wrapping the porcelain in newspaper and packing it into boxes. I decided to sell the house, although he had insisted some years before that I should keep it after he was dead. He had wanted it to remain a beacon, a lighthouse in the landscape, a point of return. But I knew it would fetch a good price. It had wonderful views.

The day before I left Bluewood, I walked through the garden for the last time. Once again, it seemed that I was at the end of something. In a spirit of rather pathetic despair, I began to consider the choices I had made, the directions I had taken, but all I could see was a series of patterns. They were the sort of intricate motifs you find on a damask cloth, or on flock wallpaper in old-fashioned hotels. You can follow the line with a finger moving forward until you reach the end of the curl, then you have to return and retrace, or hop to the next pattern which may be an inverted repetition of the last. I thought then, as I pushed the swing and watched it sway backwards and forwards under the tree, that I had no choice but to slide across to the next bunch of spiralling lines and start something new.

When I returned to my apartment there was little evidence that I had been away so long. Although I had spent over a month at Bluewood there were only two bills and one postcard stuffed into my mail box. The card, which was postmarked New York, showed a very shabby-looking Paris Opera on one side, and on the other a few lines of illegible handwriting. The only words I could make out were 'magazine', 'Anastasia' and the name of my correspondent, which I decided was Pivkin. He had added a telephone number at the bottom of his message, but that too was illegible. Even had the number been written more clearly, I would not have rung it. I thought I was finished with the Anastasias.

I slid the card behind a vase of dead flowers on the mantelpiece and forgot about it until three weeks later when my correspondant rang me.

'This is Mikhail Pivkin, you can call me Mickey,' he said when I picked up the receiver. 'The magazine gave me your number.' His voice was guttural, insinuating, vaguely pleading. 'Your Anastasias are all fakes. I know the real one. I know the real Grand Duchess.' He paused, breathing heavily down the line. 'I wrote to her yesterday, I told her about you.'

'About me?'

'I told her you could help,' he cleared his throat, coughing loudly. 'She is an old friend, I have known her many years.'

Pivkin said he was a publisher of émigré stories. 'You know: escape – danger – that sort of thing. I edited a magazine a while back. You heard of me?'

I hadn't heard of him and I wished he would go away. I had developed a bad cold, dragged it round with me for a week, and now it was at its peak. The back of my neck and shoulders ached, my nasal passages were congested, and my throat was sore.

'I got a book project for you, it's a big deal,' said Pivkin, ignoring my silence. 'We should meet up, make a date.'

Perhaps at any other time I would not have agreed to meet him, but he clung to the line, a breathy, nagging voice that I couldn't shake off without saying 'yes'. And although I knew that his Anastasia would be just as fake as all the rest, I suppose I was curious. I so rarely received telephone calls from publishers.

Since my return to the city I had sunk into a deep gloom. I sat at my desk watching the apartment grow smaller. The walls seemed to slide a few inches inwards every day and the dark furniture that the removal men had brought from Bluewood added to the claustrophobia. Then I began to feel ill and, thinking a little fresh air might help, I had opened the windows, wrapped myself in blankets, but still felt no better. I spoke to no one and missed appointments and lunch dates. All I could do was pace around the apartment shaking my head from time to time to try to shift the blocked nose. I thought my face was set in stone.

I had begun to make plans, vague ones. I called Jack, but he wasn't there. Then I wrote him a letter, resting the paper on a book of photographs that he'd bought me for my birthday. The photographs were black and white details of shiny skinned peppers and eggplants, which I didn't like much. I wrote him a long letter, tentatively suggesting a holiday. Somewhere warm, I said, picturing hot colours, imagining faint echoes in narrow streets, and sleepy afternoons. Jack had not written back, however, and he hadn't telephoned. Pivkin's invitation simply arrived at the right time.

The publisher's office was in a part of the city much further north than I had ever travelled, on the borders where the suburbs began. The road outside was deserted: there were no cars or buses and no pedestrians. Perhaps it was because of this emptiness that the pavements and gutters seemed exceptionally clean, as did the faces of the buildings and the iron fire escapes that crawled down the façades. There were no rain stains that marked the stone, no unwashed windows, no rust on the downpipes. It was as if the road and the tenements had just been constructed and one could only remark on the things that were absent. It was like an unused film set, a de Chirico street, something from a dream.

Pivkin was waiting for me in the hallway, nervous and twitching. He was an unusually pale man with a twisted smile and a tear in his creased shirt. Beyond him in the gloom was an octagonal room, a dark place made darker still by a vine that obscured the window. Pivkin shuffled towards a chair and, pushing away books and envelopes, he invited me to sit. Then he switched on a desk lamp and looked across at me, blinking, mole-like.

'They lied to you,' he said, and pointed to the magazine that lay open in front of him. It was *Twenty-Eight*, my article, the Anastasia piece. I could see the familiar images and the columns of text.

'All fakes.' He brushed the back of his hand across the page as though wiping the photographs of the women away. 'Fakes.' Then slowly he lent towards me. 'But I like the way you write, we can work together; I am a good editor, I have good contacts.' His words ended with an upward swing, and seemed to hang in the air like possibilities.

'But you want to know something about me first. You're thinking, who is this nogoodnik who promises me a Grand Duchess, who promises me a book?'

He sat down awkwardly at his desk and adjusted the feeble light so that it shone on the blotter and the bottle of ink rather than his milky face.

'You want to know something about Mickey Pivkin, huh?' And, without allowing me to answer, he continued. 'In Russia I was a student, you know, a student of languages,' he paused. 'Languages open doors to other worlds,' Pivkin said stiffly, like a child who had learnt the phrase by heart from a school book. Then he stretched out his hands, and I could see his pale fingernails fluttering like insects' wings, transparent against the light.

As a student Mikhail Pivkin had loved the physical pleasure of training his mouth to produce foreign sounds: the pouting words of French or the long, tight vowels of English. He conjugated verbs, constructed sentences, wrote essays and stories, but he was a poet at heart, he said. He liked precision, compression. He liked small things. In the evenings, before the first world war, he would stand in his apartment and read his poems aloud and, when he had finished, he would look down at his wife's smiling face. Sonia was beautiful, said Pivkin. She always wore white, moon-white with trimmings of cherry red. That was how he dreamt of her.

That was how he had dreamt of her for three years, as he marched, cleaned his boots, and brushed away the mud and blood from his uniform. He could picture her sitting by the open window in the late evening while the moths played round the lamp. Or he could see her reading, writing letters, or painting the miniature watercolour landscapes that she used to send him from time to time. At least in his dreams he had been able to share her life in some small way.

Then suddenly there wasn't time to dream any more, for out on the front line everything began to fall apart, just like the poorly-stitched seams of his overcoat. First the mail stopped coming, and then the rations and the new recruits. Then there was no more ammunition. One by one Pivkin and his friends turned back and marched home. He took rides in lorries and horse carts, but for most of the way he walked, trying to remember the sound of Sonia's voice, and anticipating how he would feel when her arms were round his neck once more. He walked towards the city, thinking about her eyes and the way her hair curled in rings over her forehead. He walked through the streets to the apartment block, picturing the beauty spot on the nape of her neck, and the small pearl-coloured scar on the back of her hand. He walked up the stairs to the front door, imagining how happy she would be to see him, but inside he found the neighbours and a priest standing next to Sonia's open coffin. She had died of hunger, Pivkin said.

He saw no reason to stay. When the coffin was buried, he turned and walked back the way he had come. The only thing to do was to keep moving. He walked across frozen estuaries and through ice forests, eating nothing but snow. He thanked God that it was cold, too cold to think about the past and the future. All that worried him were his hands, his feet and his stomach. He walked from one side of the winter right through to the other, and as the snow melted and the leaves appeared, he felt his toes again and the ends of his fingers: but he started to feel his thoughts too. Then with the spring floods came pictures in his head: the carcasses of his comrades in the trenches, the hungry children he had seen, the burnt bodies. And like a full stop at the end of a terrible list was Sonia's face, wax yellow and haggard with pain. The only thing to do was to keep moving.

On the first day that the sun began to shine, he decided to bathe in a small pond that lay at the edge of a village. He sat down on the bank and removed his boots. He peeled away his socks and, at the sight of his feet, he vomited. When he had recovered, he washed them carefully, but the gritty sand bit as it entered the wounds. Pulling his feet out of the water, he looked at the bruises and at the blood blisters glinting in the sunlight, and wondered how he could ever move on.

He rested by the side of the pond with his eyes shut and felt the sun sliding down the sky. When it began to grow colder, he heard the voice of a woman close by, murmuring to him in a language he half knew. She bound his feet with strips of cloth, helped him up and led him to her house. There she fed him strange-flavoured soups and water that never seemed to satisfy his thirst. Then she spoke to him, whispering strange incantations that made him dream of the hot sun drying his tongue and burning his lips.

After several days the fire in his brain diminished and he could see the room in which he lay, and the woman's silhouette at the end of the bed. She removed the bandages, cleaned his feet and carefully rebandaged them again. When she had finished, she came towards him and held a glass of water to his lips. He swallowed a little and then, weakly, he asked her where he was. She told him the name of the village, but it didn't help Pivkin. It was like holding a fragment of a map with one indecipherable name printed on it. He asked her the date, but she wasn't sure, and she wandered off into the yard, returning some time later with an old newspaper that had been used to wrap vegetables or meat. She pointed to the numbers at the top of the page hopefully, but Pivkin knew that wasn't right. He felt more lost than ever.

He dozed for a while, shutting out the vacuum, but when he awoke again he saw the newspaper still folded on the earth floor beside him.

This time, as his eyes cleared, he picked the paper up and began to read, translating the sentences one by one. Then he found a list of names: Nicholas, Alexandra, Alexis, Olga, Tatiana, Maria, Anastasia. And buried in the text towards the end of the column were the words 'shot dead' and 'killed by order of the Ural Soviet'.

He dropped the paper and lay back. There was a time when he might have cheered, long before, when he had sat in the mud of the trenches or as he had walked towards his home. Later, after he had buried Sonia, as his thoughts were buffeted one way and another like a screwed-up piece of paper in a windy street, he might have felt ambiva- lence, lip-biting indecision. But now, in that room where the small still things were – a shawl hanging over the back of a chair, a bowl of plums, wild flowers in a stone jar – the killing seemed so brutal and unnecessary. Now there was another set of bodies to add to the piles that were already heaped in his head. He shut his eyes and dreamt of the children – the four girls and the little boy – playing in a garden. It was like watching snatches from a fogged film, he said.

Just as Pivkin began to feel better, another man entered the house. He must have been a father, a brother or a husband: someone who owned the woman. Standing like a shadow inside the doorway, he looked at Pivkin. Then he turned towards the woman and growled. She crept to the corner where the potatoes were kept and covered her face with her hands. The man growled once more and trudged towards her. Then stretching out his huge bear paws he began to slap her head and her arms, hitting her again and again.

Pivkin, who had been crouching by the fire, got up and, taking his bag that was stashed under the mattress, he walked out of the house and the yard and the village.

Pivkin marched on. After the dark cottage he liked the movement of walking, the regularity of the paces, the ease with which he could put one foot in front of the other. He enjoyed the speed at which he could move through the landscape again.

In the second winter Pivkin met three men who were all as lost as he. The first had been a teacher in a village somewhere in the north, the second, a shopkeeper near one of the front lines. The third was a musician who had performed in cafés and restaurants before the revolution. At night, when the talk died down, the musician took a beaten violin from the bundle that he carried on his back. He had no bow, so he plucked the strings with his fingers and he sang invented songs, of lost wives hidden in walls and dead children buried under the turnip patch. The lyrics altered every night: like the men they could not settle. Once the song was sung the words floated away as weightless as ashes.

After the sadness of the songs, the men lay on the straw or the stone floor, knowing that they had left something behind: a sense of themselves, or who they used to be. All they desired was the numbness in body and mind that comes after a day's walking, or after eating and drinking, or in sleeping.

One morning they walked deep into the forest. It was a warm day, almost spring, and the sky was clear. Pivkin and the teacher sat under a patch of sunlight that fell through the leaves, and the shopkeeper, looking up at the trees, stretched his catapult ready to kill a small bird that they would roast over the fire that evening. The musician had wandered off along the track humming to himself; Pivkin could hear his voice echoing through the bracken. Then the song stopped abruptly, there was silence, and a few seconds later the musician called to them gently, as if he had seen a deer or a hare. The men edged towards him, hungry and tired. Then as they rounded the bend of the track, they saw two small girls who looked up at them, smiling and unafraid.

31

Without saying a word, the men moved towards the girls and encircled them. Pivkin stood back. He saw the pale pink scarf of the older girl pulled away, he saw it waving, he saw it drop onto the mud track. He saw the girl's yellow-white hair as they pushed her into the ditch. He saw the buttocks of the shopkeeper as he strained, labouring, into the girl. He saw the others laughing, although strangely he could hear no sounds apart from the blackbirds in the trees. Then Pivkin turned and ran away, frightened of his own complicity, scared that if he went too close he might join in. He ran away down the track, past the younger girl who stood on the ridge of grass that grew in between the ruts. He ran so fast that his lungs ached and his head grew dizzy.

He ran through the forest, tripping over undergrowth, thorns piercing his trousers and the darns in his socks. He ran through streams and rivers, and through the furrows of ploughed fields until his boots, the soles clogged with earth, began to weigh him down. He slid down slopes, skating in the slush and mud, along the tow path of a canal, past moored barges and lock-keepers cottages.

He ran on, night and day and night again, until he reached the edges of a large city. And then he stopped and, standing in the wet grass, he looked down at the river plain which was filled with lights. There were orange lights burning at windows, white lights over doorways, and yellow lights marking the lines of the streets. While he stared at the pattern of lights in front of him, Pivkin realised that he didn't want to run any more or be alone any more. He knew he wasn't strong enough for solitude, and that he was fatigued by the constant movement and dislocation. It seemed to him that each light in the river valley represented a life that was rooted and steady. That was what he wanted too. For the first time in five years Pivkin began to feel warm again.

He looked for work and was offered a night shift in an abattoir in the north eastern suburbs of the city. From midnight till morning he pulled the matted hides from the headless animals that swung towards him on hooks. He stripped their skins like a conjurer, revealing the shining membranes, the bunches of muscles and the pale networks of veins and arteries. But he hated the dripping bodies, he hated standing ankle-deep in luke-warm blood. Now he couldn't sleep, nor could he eat, for he wasn't hungry any more. His eyes began to sink deeper into his skull, his cheeks disappeared completely and his mouth, already twisted by the cold, was shut tight to hide his rotting gums.

At the end of his shift he would walk through the streets, following the routes taken by the wagons that carried the meat to market. The animals were everywhere: fragmented, diced and minced. Through the windows of the butchers' shops he could see pink peeled pig, the heads of glazed baby veal and the tongues of old cows, all decorated with flowers, tiny white roses carved from iced lard. Pivkin passed the restaurants and read the menus chalked on the slates outside: tripe, blood sausage, pigs' feet, and *tête de veau* in which one might find the thin blond eyelash of a veal calf rolled inside the meat. The city was built on the corpses of animals, thought Pivkin. They were a currency that was sucked in living, then killed, skinned, chopped, and hauled to the massive market that sprawled for acres through the heart of the city.

At night when Pivkin returned to the abattoir, he looked again at the lights in the windows of the houses and the hotels, but they had taken on another complexion. They were cold, mocking and smug.

On the worst days, he would go to church. He hadn't been to mass since he was a child pulled there by his mother, her hand gripping his. Now Pivkin would stand at the back and follow the prayers. It was good, he said, to hear his own fragile voice blending with the others, he began to feel part of something again. After the service, Pivkin watched the groups of men on the church steps. They talked together while they waited for their wives who were still praying or lighting candles inside the church. These men were tall and well fed, and their voices were clear and strong. As Pivkin listened to their conversations he recalled words and phrases that he had forgotten, polite greetings and endearments, words with weight that stayed where they were put. He realised then that he was tired of spending his days alone and his nights in the presence of the dead animals. He wanted his voice to mingle with the voices of the men on the church steps. He wanted to feel like he really belonged somewhere again.

Each week after mass, Pivkin would move a little closer towards the men until one afternoon he was standing right at the bottom of the steps. It was growing dark and cold and the men stamped their feet and blew on their hands to keep warm. Then there was a sudden noise from the street, a car backfired, someone shouted, and the men turned their heads. At that moment one of them looked down and saw Pivkin's face staring up. For a few seconds the man stared back, then he smiled and stretched out his hand. It was a gesture that almost made Pivkin weep.

He joined them on the steps, but was too shy to talk. He could only stutter and grunt, and look down at his boots. It was a month before he was able to put one word in front of the other and make simple phrases. Then slowly, between Christmas and the New Year, the thin trickle of words turned into a stream of sentences, growing longer and more complex as the weeks passed. First he told them about the war, then about his wife and the walk through the snow. Finally he described the animals and the abattoir.

'I'm looking for another job,' he said hopefully. 'Do you know of anything?'

The men looked at Pivkin's crooked face, his shuffling feet, his rotting teeth, and they shook their heads. They patted his back in friendship or sympathy and they turned away.

THE SHOP

'It's strange how things happen,' said Pivkin, as he pulled the blind over the darkened window. 'Odd.'

He sat back in his chair and stroked the pages of the magazine again. 'Some weeks later, just as the rain was beginning, a man stopped me in the street. He gripped my arm, opened my clenched fist and gave me a used metro ticket. Written on the back, in tiny writing, was the name and address of the shop.'

'The shop,' said Pivkin, leaning towards me over the desk, 'I must explain the shop. If you take a map of the city, put your finger on the abattoir in the north, then draw a diagonal line downwards to the other side, you will find the shop. The abattoir and the shop are diametrically opposed. Polarities. It would take almost a whole day to walk from one side of the city to the other,' said Pivkin. 'A whole day to walk from the abattoir to the shop.'

The shop was double-fronted and painted blue. At the entrance was a guardian, a straight-limbed, narrow-eyed boy named Kots who wore black and gold livery cut from an old soldier's uniform. If you approached the door Kots would pull it wide open and the daylight fell on the pale green walls. You would see that the shop was a place of magic, of spells whispered over coloured velvets and brocades, of enchanted patterns in beads and sequins. Displayed on the shelves and in the glass cabinets and the glass-fronted drawers were bags, silk scarves, sashes, gloves and hats. There were accessories of every sort covered with small stitched butterflies and birds, silver scarab beetles and silk-painted caterpillars. There were jungles of trees from which the spangled faces of monkeys appeared. There were tiger stripes in the flat-stitch undergrowth. There were knot-stitch snakes. And there were flowers: marigolds, snap dragons, foxgloves and larkspur, all picked out in floss flax or flourishing thread of moss green and rosewood brown.

If you asked Nicole, she might show you the little skull caps made from copper-coloured lace, or the evening turbans plumed with feathers. She would take you to the oval mirror and she would place the hat over your hair, tilting it left or right with her small hands. Lina would pull the gloves from the drawers and unwrap them from the tissue paper. She would let you touch the silk stitches, the chain and daisy, seed and satin stitch that ran between the fingers and up the arms. From a glass case, Olga might take out a pair of slippers and hold them up to the light. Or she would tell you how lovely you looked with the salmon scarf wound round your neck. And with a flick of her fingers she would tweak the silk so that the perfect pearl, scales of the leaping fish could be glimpsed in between the folds.

But Pivkin saw none of this. At least not at first.

On the night before his interview Pivkin cleaned his boots and brushed down his jacket. He trimmed the translucent hair that had grown over his forehead, and he clipped his finger nails. Then, early in the morning before the sun rose, Pivkin set out, walking steadily through the streets.

As the eastern city gave way to the west he noticed the transformation. There were gold mansions with silver roofs, and emerald gardens dotted with flowers. On these streets the windows of the eating houses were veiled with green velvet or cotton lace, and the butchers were hidden down side roads or set back in courtyards. Only the cake shops and chocolate shops displayed their goods, stacked like jewels on stands and glass shelves. In this part of the city everyone was beautiful. There were ladies with skin as smooth as a milk opal, and gentlemen with hair and whiskers that shone with perfumed oil.

By the time Pivkin reached the back entrance to the shop, he began to think that his search for a job was a hopeless waste of time. He felt too ugly to work in such surroundings, for even the square dark courtyard, where the dustbins were kept, seemed elegant. Pivkin stood in the shadow and brushed down his suit and combed his thin hair with his fingers, then he made his way, doubtfully, towards the back door of the building.

Sitting on a low stool in the entrance was a surly man called Dandy, the size of a small child. At his feet was a melancholy dog. They both looked up when Pivkin approached and he was certain that he saw them scowl. Then, tripping over every word, Pivkin explained why he had come, but it was only when he produced the old metro ticket from his pocket that the concierge would let him in.

Pivkin was led through a kitchen, a narrow corridor and then up the back stairs to the workshop. This was a large room and, despite the greyness of the day, the light flooded over the rounded backs of the girls who sat at tables and frames sewing patterns onto silk. Those girls were the daughters of politicians and aristocrats, or the offspring of dressmakers from St Petersburg. One of them had been employed as a ladies' maid in a Moscow palace and another had lived in a convent in the Urals. They all sat diligently at the frames in their smocks of beige linen, and on their heads were caps, which the pretty ones had pushed back so that their faces could be seen. There was only one girl whose cap was pulled right down so that her eyes were hidden in its shadow.

At one side of the workshop was the staircase that led up to the attic where the girls slept, and beyond this was the office of the work mistress. Madame Hortense was a thin woman with a face that looked as if the flesh of her cheeks had been scooped out with a dessertspoon. Her tight-bodiced dress reached the floor, and her hair was tied into a chignon, like a spiral clamped to the back of her head. She greeted Pivkin coldly, told him to sit, and asked him inconsequential things about his background and his family. She tested his handwriting and listened to him speak English, French, German and Russian. Then she told him to add and subtract, multiply and divide. She did not look at him, she ignored his face, his battered, frosted skin, his misshapen features. The only parts of Pivkin at which she stared were his hands, scrubbed clean of blood that morning. She seemed to approve of their condition for she nodded and said, 'You have good hands, Monsieur Pivkin.' Then after a short pause she continued, 'You will begin work tomorrow morning at 8.30.'

Pivkin's days slipped pleasantly into routine. Each morning, installed at a small desk in Madame's office, he would reply to enquiries in his best hand. He was attentive to the margins and the space between the lines, and he carefully curled the letters with a dip pen. The work was not difficult, and from time to time he would lift his head, as if deep in thought, and watch the needlewomen in the workshop. They fascinated him, for each one was unique. It had been a long time since he had seen such fresh faces: bright and unblemished. He would watch the girls as Madame inspected their work and as Andrei Nikolaevich advised them on the patterns they were to sew. The artist was a thin, pockmarked man, a weeping willow who smothered his skin and hair with scented powder. His suits were of velvet, lichen-yellow and birch-tree grey, but they too were muted by dust. He left a trail of it wherever he went, over the drawings that he had sketched, or the floorboards on which he had stood. It was like a cloud of sadness, thought Pivkin, like desiccated tears. Even when he spoke, which he did in gentle whispers, puffs of powder would emanate from his mouth.

After lunch, Pivkin worked in the store room, arranging buttons, beads and pearls, and assessing the lengths of silk, under the supervision of Boris Dagarov. Dagarov seemed at his happiest when each item was counted and placed safely in the appropriate drawer, and when the order papers, with their duplicates and triplicates, had been filed. He was an impressive man, as tall as the highest shelf in the store room, hair as black as Madame's dresses, and a moustache as heavy as a raven's wings.

Only one thing marred his looks, for at some time his jaw had been broken and reset badly. In consequence his chin appeared to be sliding to the right, but despite this the girls still thought he was handsome. He was also admired, it seemed, for his back-slapping humour that he shared with everyone but Kots.

'Came from nowhere,' said Dagarov to Pivkin one afternoon as they were rolling up the red China silk. 'Doesn't smell right, always listening, always watching, never says a word.'

And it was true, there was something about Kots, his small eyes, his soft cat-footed silence.

'As slimy as a young trout,' said Dagarov, brushing away the silk threads that were clinging to his dust coat.

It was perhaps because of Boris Dagarov's distrust of Kots that he was so careful with the contents of the store room, for he was always checking the drawers and boxes, and measuring the lengths of material, heedful of waste. Even the smallest fragment of cloth or ribbon was shut away, to be made into fabric roses or peonies that were destined for the decoration of a hat or the collar of a dress. Dagarov was good at his job.

In the evenings, after supper, the men retired to the basement where they slept. It was comfortable down there, warm, not too damp. Dagarov had appropriated a leather buttonback armchair and a large red Persian carpet, and he had arranged them in the centre of the room, giving the basement the air of a gentlemen's club. Most evenings, before going to bed, he would sit in his chair and roll cigarettes, smoking them one after another, while Dandy sorted through his bunches of keys. On the other side of the room, Kots would write in a small black notebook. Pivkin, however, would simply lie on his bed with his hands behind his head, thinking about the needlewomen. He would picture each one, considering the turn of Valentina's nose, the brightness of Ludmilla's eyes or the pitiful smile on Vera's lips. Occasionally he would consult Dagarov, but the store room manager was no poet and could only contemplate the thrust of Lara's breasts or the width of Luba's hips.

In the months that followed, Pivkin thawed completely. His face lost the tense frozen look he had carried with him for years. The blood pumped round his body again and even the tips of his fingers and toes felt warm. He had never been happier; he had fallen in love. The girl was called Anna, although everyone in the workshop referred to her as 'the seamstress' because she never responded to her real name. She was a strange and silent girl. Dagarov said that in the convent she had been beaten by soldiers. The men had attacked the nuns with bayonets, leaving them for dead in the entrance to the church. It was for this reason, said Dagarov, that she was mute. The memory of those violent words, shouted as the rifle butt had hit her face, were so brutal and so clear that she could no longer stand the sound of her mother tongue.

The seamstress was a humourless girl, her mouth a thin straight line across her face, her throat and jaw scarred, and her fingers bent and crooked At night she slept in the darkest shadows of the attic and during the day her place was in the dimmest corner of the workshop. When it was time to eat she would sit at the end of the kitchen table and slowly nibble, squirrel-like, whatever had been placed before her. She was given the most menial chores – the sewing of seams or the making of buttonholes – but despite the dullness of these tasks, her work was still fine and her stitches even.

She was not the prettiest girl, far from that. Her face, or what one could see of it, seemed shattered and her hands and arms were strangely scarred. The seamstress reminded Pivkin of the small damaged things that he had witnessed on his journey: the beaten woman who had cared for him so carefully in her hut, or the girl in the forest with the fine hair of a small child. She reminded him of the frozen birds he had seen in the north and the dead rabbits he had eaten in the south. She reminded him of the limbs of the baby lambs in the abattoir and of his wife's bruised eyes inside the frilled coffin. She reminded him of all the broken things, of his own complicity in the breakages, and his inability to stop the damage. He felt a terrible guilt and an over-whelming compassion.

As he watched the seamstress working, he began to sense a shift, like spring into summer, a heat that filled him. At meal times he tried to sit next to her and often he would follow her in the early evening, when the girls were permitted to leave the building. He watched her limping shuffle and the mournfulness in her shoulders as she walked along the river bank. He kept his distance, however, careful that she did not see him, for he was bashful and confused about his love.

There were times on those walks when he was sure that he himself was followed, certain that he had seen the gold streak of Kots' uniform dart behind a tree or a dark hedge. Did Kots know of his evening walks? Had he told the others? These thoughts ate at Pivkin. He gnawed at his fingernails when he saw Kots in the basement writing in his notebook.

He was relieved when the girl changed direction one evening. Instead of wandering through the narrow park, she turned away from the river towards the Russian Orthodox church, still ignorant of Pivkin trailing behind her. When the sun set on warm evenings like this, he waited in the corner of the church courtyard while she slipped inside and lit a candle that illuminated the dark walls. After she left, he could smell the melting honey wax heavy in the air.

The summer was hot, an itching heat that was humid and uncomfortable. The walls of the workshop seemed to seep perspiration. The stiff satins and the starched cottons grew limp, and the girls' damp fingers left marks on the precious Italian damasks and brocades. In the windowless store room, Dagarov worried about lost buttons and bent needles. He picked fussily at the threads that stuck to his hands, and pushed away a sweaty lock of hair from his forehead.

Madame became exacting. She scolded the girls for shoddy work, pulling out embroidered stitches and cursing the needlewomen as she did so. Each day her irritation grew, until one afternoon when the sun was at its highest, she caught sight of the seamstress's fingers and the cotton fabric she held between them. Snatching the cloth from the girl, Madame held it close to her eyes and inspected the seams, then she threw it across the table, spitting words at the girl. Perhaps the heat was too much for Madame Hortense. Perhaps her dress was too heavy or her hairpins were pulling the skin too tightly at the back of her head, because the girl's seams were as precise and the stitches as even as ever.

The seamstress wept. She had only half understood the machine-gun tirade which shot from Madame's mouth, but she recognised the ugly tone and the staccato beat. She wept, her head in her hands, her shoulders moving in time to her sobs. Nothing could stop the flow. No kind words could halt the tears that ran over the girl's smock and onto the floorboards. The seamstress sobbed so much that she could not eat and was sent to bed with a glass of milk, which she did not drink. The girl cried all night, muffling the sounds she made with her pillow, and in the morning her eyes were so red and swollen she could hardly see.

All day the seamstress cried, soaking her dress. Then the tears began to run down her stockinged legs and fall into the cracks between the floor boards. There were so many tears that Dagarov worried that the plaster ceiling of the shop would become stained by them, and that the tears would begin to drip onto the embroidered gloves and silk bags that were displayed below. Pivkin tried to talk to the girl, whispering gentle words, but she didn't respond and simply held her head in her battered hands.

By the second evening the seamstress's tears had dried enough for her to swallow some soup and when she had finished, she left the shop quietly. Pivkin watched her from an upstairs window, a small bent figure on the opposite side of the road. He waited five minutes and then he followed her. He knew where she was going.

She must have prayed a long time, for as he stood outside the Russian church he watched the residue of the sunlight moving behind the low roofs. Then everything turned grey: the stone of the church, the gravel in the courtyard and the plants that grew in the window boxes on the other side of the street. He wiped the perspiration from his face with the back of his hand, and shuffled his feet from side to side in the gravel dust.

Just as he was thinking of leaving, she appeared on the steps again, blowing her nose with a handkerchief that she had pulled from her pocket. She looked straight ahead, listening to the evening sounds that came from the apartments and the street. Then quickly, more quickly than Pivkin had ever seen her move, she descended the steps, ran across the yard to the gate and down the street towards the shop.

This time the girl had lit six candles. When Pivkin looked inside the church, there were six small flames wobbling in the dark. This time he too lit a candle. For his dead wife or for the seamstress – he wasn't sure.

It was almost night when he left the church. He stood on the steps, wondering what the seamstress had thought, what she had seen. He looked at the windows opposite, the curling pattern of the church gates, the gravel path that led to the steps. And as he looked, he saw, at the edge of his eye, a white fleck, a folded piece of paper lying on the ground by his left foot. Pivkin bent down slowly, picked it up and unfolded it in his hand. It was a photograph dampened by her tear-soaked handkerchief, but all that Pivkin could distinguish in the moonlight were five silhouettes against a background of white.

Later, sitting on his bed, he saw a smudged family group: a man in uniform and four girls in the snow. It was a snapshot, with a small tear in one corner. On the back, in black ink, was the word *Papa* and the initials *OTMA*. He had known the man's face all his life. Even in this creased image Pivkin could recognise him – not so much by the features, but by the cut of the beard, the tilt of the cap, and the way he seemed to lean sideways into the photograph. He thought he recognised the girls too, but perhaps that was because there were four of them. Four princesses. Then he looked at the smallest girl more carefully. Her hair was tucked up inside her hat, and her mouth was a straight line across her face. Pivkin was certain that he knew her.

Everyone had heard the rumours, that the Tsar hadn't been shot, but was hidden in an ice palace in the North, and that the four Grand Duchesses, saved from the bullets by the jewels that had been sewn into their corsets, were now the concubines of a rich man in China. Then the pretenders had started to turn up; men who swore that they were really the Tsar, and deluded peasant boys each claiming that he was the heir to the Russian throne. And then there were the girls in the East, each of whom maintained that she was the youngest daughter, carried by palace servants across the border to safety.

All night Pivkin thought, and his thoughts shimmered between belief and disbelief. Perhaps the photograph was really a postcard, reproduced in thousands for servant girls and their mistresses to buy, the sort of thing that could have been purchased anywhere in the capital before the revolution. But the image that was folded in his trouser pocket was too flimsy, there was no photographer's mark on the back, and the pose was quite unlike those formal royal photographs that he had seen throughout his childhood.

Was the round-faced child in the photograph really the seamstress? But there were so many girls that looked like that, thought Pivkin. In certain lights, all the needlewomen in the workshop might resemble the girl. And if the seamstress *were* the daughter of the Tsar, why was she hiding in a shop? Perhaps she had stolen the photograph, or perhaps she had been given it by an exiled royal employee. Perhaps it simply belonged to somebody else.

At breakfast Pivkin handed her the photograph, expecting her to refuse it, to shake her head and say that it wasn't hers. Without saying a word, she took it, however, and pushed it back into her pocket. This was the first time she had looked him in the eye and it was as if she were searching for something from him.

He approached her several times that day. He whispered questions in her ear as she bent over the sewing frame, but she did not answer. She did not even turn round. Her refusal to confide in him angered Pivkin. He wanted to help her, and yet it seemed that she did not trust him. His love for her began to have an edge to it, a little bitterness. Unable to contain his frustration, he banged the button drawers and dropped the rolls of silk onto the *atelier* table with a bump. He even considered telling Dagarov or even worse, Kots, just to spite the girl, but by the time he met them in the basement his anger had subsided.

All through the summer Pivkin searched for photographs and postcards of the dead Imperial family. He purchased them from the men who sold second-hand books on the quay. Then he stuck all the images into an album bought specially for the purpose, which he hid beneath his mattress in the basement. At night when he was alone, Pivkin would study the pictures trying to memorise the girl's features, and in the morning he would mentally measure the seamstress's face for similarities. His album consisted mostly of watercolour images of the family, their faces smoothed until they were unrecognisable, or dull prints in which the Grand Duchesses were obscured by a smudge of shadow here and a patch of light there. But no matter how many pictures Pivkin collected, in each photograph the youngest girl seemed different. He could not pin her down for, unlike her father, there was nothing distinctive about her at all. She still possessed the unformed face of a child.

The hot summer was replaced by a dreary, sluggish autumn. Lina left to marry a man who worked as a bank cashier in the provinces and was given a wedding gift of a pair of fine silk gloves, with love birds embroidered on the backs of the hands. Then two of the needlewomen found employment in a couture house that had opened several streets away. They whispered to the others that the pay was better, and the conditions less strict. They said that embroidery was old-fashioned, and that the clothes that Mademoiselle designed were plainer, simpler and more modern.

Their words seemed to act like a prophecy for in the weeks that followed, the shop was quiet, and neither Lina nor the workshop girls were replaced. In his studio, Andrei Nikolaevich continued to draw, and in the workshop the girls continued to sew, but the belts and embroidered collars and gloves were folded between sheets of tissue paper and left in a pile in the corner of the room. These were long weeks, when the oblique sun projected purple shadows over the needlewomen as they worked. The light was weak by four o'clock, the saddest time of the day, and the girls were permitted to stop sewing and drink tea and talk amongst themselves. The lack of work, which at first had been a novelty, now made the women anxious. They grew restless, looking for small tasks to undertake in the late hours of the afternoon. Even the seamstress appeared distracted. On several occasions Pivkin caught her looking out of the window, staring at the top of Kots' motionless head as he stood by the front door to the shop.

The lull in the work ended in December when the customers slowly began to return, looking for presents for their sisters, daughters and nieces. In the week before Christmas the shop was so busy that the needlewomen were sent down to help Nicole and Olga with the wrapping of gifts. The seamstress was the most adept at present wrapping. Her fingers were small and nimble and she cut the paper with a rapidity never seen before. The corners of the wrapped items were as neat as the sheets on a hospital bed; the knots and bows she tied with the silver-blue ribbons were both practical and decorative.

At first the seamstress was reluctant to descend the front stairs that led to the shop. She did not want to remove her dust coat or her cap, and only did so after persuasion from Madame. Pivkin thought she looked smaller and frailer in her skirt and blouse. The scars that had been hidden by the collar of the linen smock were now visible, running like a seam down the side of her neck. And he hadn't seen her red gold hair before, which in the winter light seemed to possess the same painted quality as the postcards he had stuck into his album. Pivkin sat in the office with the door open, catching glimpses of the seamstress as she smoothed down her skirt. He kept looking up from his paperwork to check the distance from her forehead to her nose, or from her ears to her jawbone.

Downstairs she stood behind a table which was beneath the stairs. She never once looked up, neither at the customers nor at the other shop girls. Cutting stretches of paper ready for the boxed scarves and sashes, she ignored the gossip of the ladies who floated amongst the hat stands and the carved wooden hands on which the gloves were displayed.

On the day before Christmas Eve the seamstress was still rooted in the darkness of the stairs, folding and pleating the paper with a sureness that was surprising in such a timid girl. It was a clear day and the thin sunlight pierced the clouds and entered the shop like faint torch beams. The low light inched round the room all morning, high-lighting the details on a drawstring bag, or the thread-veined cheeks of an elderly customer. At eleven o'clock it lit up the golden figures stitched onto an evening shawl, and just before lunch the light hit the table of the seamstress. At first it was simply a narrow streak that gently stroked her fingers as she tied a bow around a package, then the clouds must have parted completely, for as Olga said later, 'it was as if someone had switched on a light.'

The light was as strong as a spotlight in the theatre. It was so bright it caught the seamstress, illuminating her face as she lifted it up to the warmth. For the first time in three days she looked up and, at that instant, from somewhere deep in the shop came a loud scream.

Fearing an accident, Pivkin ran to the top of the stairs and looked down. The women, like characters in an old-fashioned melodrama, were frozen in a *tableau*. They stood, immobile, turned towards a young woman in a pale blue coat and a fur hat. She had one gloved hand over her mouth, the other hand stretched out, pointing at the seamstress. Pivkin could see that Kots had pulled the door wide open and was now standing inside the shop. Like the customers, he too stared at the blue lady, his lips slightly parted in anticipation.

The silence was broken by a woman standing in a far corner of the room. Fumbling in her pocket she took out a pair of spectacles and placed them on her bony nose. Then, looking from the astonished lady in blue to the blank face of the seamstress, she cried, 'Imperial Highness, Imperial Highness.' She ran towards the girl, knelt down and kissed the hem of the seamstress's grey serge skirt.

The rest was confusion. The women pressed around the table, and the seamstress was pushed right back into the corner under the stair-case. Kots, however, was still standing at the entrance to the shop. He seemed to hesitate for a few seconds, his hand clutching the round brass door knob, then he closed the door softly behind him and disappeared down the street.

They took the seamstress away that afternoon. From the workshop windows the needlewomen watched the blue-coated lady with her arm around the girl, followed by her elderly servant. Afterwards, when Nicole came upstairs to pack the seamstress's things, she told Pivkin and Dagarov that the lady was a Countess and had been a friend of the Imperial family; her companion had been a housemaid in the palace. The seamstress had been invited to stay with them for Christmas and then she would be taken to England or Denmark to be reunited with her family.

'Just like a fairy tale,' said Nicole as she climbed the stairs.

Christmas was quiet. The girls, Madame and Andrei Nikolaevich had left to celebrate the holiday with relatives or friends. Only Dagarov, Pivkin and Kots remained in the shop. Dandy had wandered off, with his dog, to the rough lands at the edge of the city, where his circus friends had parked their caravans and pitched their tents.

The building was quiet. The streets were quiet – too quiet for Pivkin. He walked along the boulevards, thoughts knotting in his head. He felt straightforward emotions: triumph in being right, and anger with himself for falling in love with a Grand Duchess, but he also felt profound sadness, for he knew he would never see her again.

On Christmas Eve, Pivkin bought a bottle of wine, drank most of it, then lay on his bed sinking into a depression deeper than he had ever experienced. He had never felt like this before, not even on the day he had discovered his dead wife in her coffin. Then he had been numbed, but now his feelings were fresh and new again, as tender as cherry blossom that had been bruised and crushed. He turned over and tried to sleep. He would never see her again. He would never be as close to her as he had been, never be able to whisper words in her ears, never be able to watch the scars on her fingers as she worked. He could of course continue to collect the photographs that he found in the newspapers and magazines. There would be scores of books written too. He could follow her life at a distance, her marriage, her children. He could watch her grow old and die once more.

Pivkin slept, although his sleep was interrupted by dreams which, when he awoke, briefly embarrassed and shamed him. He dreamt of kissing the seamstress, bending towards her and pressing his lips against hers. Then he must have muddled her with the beaten women and the forest girl, for he dreamt bad things, and finally he saw her funeral. The procession was led by a bird that goose-stepped ahead of the coffin, its bronze feathers swaying as it marched. Pivkin followed the other mourners, each one dressed in hooded gowns of white silk, embroidered with ivy that tangled over them like a web.

The thud of the coffin as it hit the bottom of the trench woke him and, after collecting his thoughts, he looked across at snoring Dagarov. Then he turned over and noticed that Kots' bed was empty. It had been stripped, his mattress rolled, and placed on the bare wire-netting of the bed base was his neatly folded uniform. The small wooden box that the boy had kept under his bed was still there, but the lid was wide open and when Pivkin got up and looked inside he saw that it was empty.

He spent the rest of the day walking by the river, his mouth furred from too much wine the night before. The veins in his forehead felt as if they were plucked like the strings of a double bass; they vibrated long, deep, regular beats inside his head. The sound of his feet as he crossed the gravel paths said 'Kots and the seamstress', 'the seamstress and Kots'. He sat for hours on a park bench, just to stop the noise. Then, to make things worse, when he finally returned to the shop, he was greeted at the door by a gendarme.

Apparently the seamstress had disappeared. She had left the house of the Countess and had not come back. The river flowed at the bottom of the garden and the police were posted on the bridges to check for floating bodies. They were worried for the girl. She was weak and disturbed; anything could have happened.

On their return, the needlewomen shook their heads, and whispered stories to each other of the girl's strangeness, and how they had always known that she was mad. Then the doorman's absence was reported and Dagarov claimed that Kots was a murderer. He said that the boy must have strangled the seamstress and had dumped her body in the river, or he had taken her back home where she would be put on trial and executed. Pivkin listened to his accusations, but he found it difficult to imagine a murderer who folded his uniform and piled it neatly on his stripped bed before he went off to commit the deed.

In the early spring of the following year, the Countess's companion returned to the shop to look for an embroidered handkerchief for her niece. As she was shown the designs – the white buttonhole scallops, the rounded-rose scallops and the raised satin-stitch flowers – she told Olga and Nicole that she had never been certain that the seamstress was a Grand Duchess after all. There was something wrong about the way the girl walked, the way she held her head. 'And she never uttered a word,' said the old servant. 'Not like our Anastasia.'

By Easter they had forgotten her, all of them except Pivkin.

'She just went missing,' he said, sliding his hand through his pale hair. 'She disappeared, I never saw her again.'

PIVKIN'S PROPOSITION

Pivkin got up and switched on the light. I saw his contorted face, the grotesque knots of the vine across the window and his bleak little office. On his desk was the copy of my article.

'We've found her,' he said. 'We've found the seamstress after all this time.' He pulled open a drawer and took out a bottle and some glasses. 'Dagarov found her.'

Pivkin poured two drinks and handed me one across the desk.

'Here's to Boris Dagarov.' He threw the liquor into his mouth and swallowed, a dribble of white vodka trailing down his chin. Wiping his mouth with the back of his hand he said, 'I told him to find her. It took him thirty five years, but he did it.'

It was in the winter of 1939 that Boris Dagarov saw the seamstress again. He was standing at the edge of a cross roads, when he noticed her peering out of the window of a passing bus. Recognising her face instantly, Dagarov ran towards the bus stop, but as he reached out for the metal pole to pull himself aboard, the bus moved off and the seamstress's face disappeared. The following day he travelled the bus line from its beginning to its end, descending at every stop and waiting in case he should see her. He mingled with the crowds and stared at one female face after another. Then he questioned shopkeepers, flower sellers and street cleaners, but no one had seen the thin-lipped, narrow-nosed seamstress.

Deciding to widen his search, Dagarov drew a map of the city and on it he marked the bus stops and the roads that he had already surveyed. Then he consulted the bus timetable and made a note of all the corresponding buses. Over the next few months he followed the lines he had drawn on his map, creating a web across the city. He visited places that he had never seen before, searching systematically day and night.

When the Germans came in the June of 1940, the streets emptied, and now Dagarov saw the faces watching *him*. There were frightened faces that peered out from behind curtains, and glaring faces of soldiers that scrutinised him as he passed. He decided to postpone his search, and took down his home-made map that had been pinned on the back of the bedroom door. Only occasionally did he scan the people who stood in shop queues or those who had been rounded up by the police. Then in the dreadful summer of 1942, he ran his eyes discreetly along the lines of women and children who were waiting to be taken to the velodrome, but the seamstress wasn't amongst them.

At the end of the war, Dagarov wandered towards the railway stations and watched the returning refugees. As he inspected the mass of drained vacant faces that passed him, he realised, however, that his search for the seamstress was almost hopeless. It seemed impossible to him then that one fragile Russian woman could have survived the war.

He left the city soon afterwards and moved south to a town perched on a rocky hill. There he worked in the basement of the town hall, sorting death certificates into the narrow drawers of a wooden cabinet. But even in the filing office he couldn't forget the seamstress. In the late afternoon her face would peer out at him from the shadows in the corners of the room.

Returning to the city ten years later, Dagarov decided to begin his search again, but this time he treated it with less urgency. His hunt for the seamstress became a hobby, something that he did on Saturday and Sunday afternoons when the sun was high. Making no plans, drawing no maps, he simply zigzagged across the city from left to right, examining the names on letter boxes and on shop fronts. He found it was almost a pleasure to wander into those parts of the city that he did not know.

Then, quite by chance, he saw her again: the same tired face and the same small sad features. The seamstress was sitting at a window, her fingers feeding a strip of cloth under the needle of a sewing machine. Pins were held between her pursed lips.

'She does alterations,' Pivkin told me. 'Takes up hems and mends holes. Dagarov says her hands are so worn she cannot hold a needle any more. He says her eyesight is going.' Leaning towards me, Pivkin paused. 'I want to help her,' he said. 'You see, I feel for her still, after all this time.' He grasped the top pocket of his shirt and tugged at it as if his heart were beating fast underneath. 'I said to Dagarov that we must help her, but I haven't any money, this is all I can do,' Pivkin held out his shaking hands to the room. 'You see this is why I ask you.'

He looked down at the magazine in front of him.

'I like your writing. You could help her. You understand what it was like,' he sighed. 'I thought we could write an article,' he touched the pages and his hand stroked the faces in the photographs. 'I thought you could write an article, then we could make a book. You could write it for her, write her memoirs.'

'A ghost writer,' I said, although the words caught slightly in my sore throat, and Pivkin cupped his hand around his ear as if he hadn't heard. 'A ghost writer,' I said again more clearly.

'A ghost writer.' He pushed the words around his mouth and looked pleased with my suggestion. 'Yes, that's good.'

'So you're commissioning me to write her memoirs?'

He bowed his head, looked away and smiled slightly.

'Maybe not so much a commission, I see it more like this . . .' his fingers began to draw invisible patterns over the columns of text, and I thought I saw his eyes, under their heavy lids, surveying me just as the fake Grand Duchesses had done. 'We make a contract. You go, you interview her, and then you write the book. When it's finished, I help you publish it, as an agent maybe. We go somewhere big, Random House, then I take a tiny percentage. Or maybe if you don't like that, we can negotiate a small introduction fee before you leave. You see, I'm giving you the story, it's almost a gift.' He lifted his face and looked at me carefully.

'And what does the seamstress get out of all this?'

'Madame,' said Pivkin gravely, 'she can never go back to her family as she is. They will never accept her now, but maybe with the book she will become celebrated. There will be interviews. She will be invited to parties. Maybe she can find a lawyer. You see there is unclaimed money that belongs to the family. This book is like. . . how can we say. . .' he rubbed his hand across his forehead, 'public relations, it is like public relations. You will do very well, it will be a success for you.'

'But why don't you go yourself? Why don't you write the book?'

'My heart,' and once again he gripped the top pocket of his shirt. 'I am not well. I cannot travel. And I like the way you write. You have a reputation as a writer, I believe. She will talk better to a woman I think.' He looked up at me, smiling broadly this time.

I was cold. I put my coat around my shoulders.

'Think about it,' said Pivkin. 'Take your time.'

He offered me another drink which I refused, then led me into the hallway and out of the door.

'Think about it,' he said again, putting his small white hand on my shoulder. 'Let me know,' and he turned round and slid back into the dark.

THE BOX OF PHOTOGRAPHS

Despite the fact that I took neither Mikhail Pivkin, nor his seamstress, entirely seriously, there were moments when I imagined the city he had described and I found myself wandering along the paths that edged the river, or the wide streets that led to the church. Then slowly, I began to connect Pivkin's story with a hundred half-remembered stories of my own.

At first, I saw icicles gripping the underside of the eaves of the white house at Bluewood, and afternoons of long blue shadows in the garden. Then there was the image of a palm tree waving insistently in the sea breeze, followed by the blue-green domes of a Russian Orthodox church.

I did not pursue Pivkin's proposition, however. Naively, I had not expected to pay for the information. I had not envisaged a contract or an introduction fee, and it was because of this that I tried to dismiss his story from my head. I remember now, that there were other, less tangible catalysts that propelled me towards the decision I took that winter. It seems ironic that it is always those small, seemingly insignificant incidents that ultimately drive one forward.

After my meeting with Pivkin the snow began. For three weeks it fell, thick ice flakes blown by sea winds. It seemed to freeze everything it touched, not only the earth and the roads, but the people as well. They were as stiff as lead soldiers, standing at bus stops and in movie queues waiting for a thaw. The wind was biting; it gnawed at my skin and made my eyes weep. Every year it seemed to get worse.

About that time, I was asked to undertake a series of short interviews for a fashion magazine. My first subject was a writer I admired. I had read all his work and enjoyed the quiet politeness of his prose. He was a tall man in his fifties who appeared charmingly unaware or unconcerned by his fame. I had seen him occasionally from a distance, at parties and book launches and I was, I suppose, attracted to him.

I had planned the interview carefully, hoping to impress him, but the questions I posed in the restaurant that December afternoon only provoked monosyllabic replies. He looked at me briefly, slipping his eyes over my face and returning them to his plate, then lifting them again to watch the diners behind me. Like everyone I met in those days, he seemed suspicious and guarded, offering no more than a few short sentences on the problems of creativity, of finding the time to write or of searching for ideas. I thought that perhaps he was shy, but in truth, he was probably irritated by my incessant chatter and resented my bright glib briskness.

When I had finished my questions, we sat in silence looking at the snowflakes drifting like torn paper, and I realised that there was nothing else to say. A barrier had installed itself across the lunch table that was as thick as the snow outside. We didn't order dessert or coffee. The interview was at an end when the empty plates were taken away. He asked for the bill, escorted me to the door and we shook hands in the cold. I walked away down the street feeling disappointed and alone.

I was very alone that winter. Despite the Christmas cards and invitations that I received almost daily, I felt adrift and isolated. I didn't go out much and became careless about my appearance, evading the mirror in the bathroom and forgetting to brush my hair which had grown lank. I wore the same clothes every day – a sweater and a pair of wide slacks. It was easier to pull on those old things already softened by dirt than to thrust my hand into the closet and pull out something rigid and cold. In the mornings I would sit, half dressed, at the type-writer and tap slowly at the keys, pushing out the article, letter by letter, filling in the blanks and the silences with inventions of my own. I was good at that.

Occasionally there were other interviews that saved me from my dreary self. The prospect of meeting new people at least forced me to wash my hair again and iron a skirt and blouse. I still avoided the mirror, however, and would go without make-up to the rendezvous, pulling the collar of my coat up round my chin and hiding the rest of my face with a low brimmed hat. My interviewees were not all as uncommunicative as the first. Sometimes they talked a great deal, but our conversations seemed to slide over a surface as smooth and as thin as ice. As soon as my companions felt the ice give and thought that they might be slipping into deep water, they glided swiftly away towards another, safer topic.

But each new assignment, however frustrating, was a way of delaying decisions. The money from the sale of the house in Bluewood had come through and it was a considerable sum, a large solid lump in my bank account. As I sat dreaming by the typewriter, staring blankly out of the windows edged with fern frost, I could see the figures flashing tantalisingly at me every now and then. I swayed between placing the capital carefully and living off the interest, as I had been advised to do, or using the money to finance a long journey. I began to see my new wealth as a means of levering myself out of that white coldness.

In the letter I had sent to Jack two weeks before my meeting with Pivkin, I had suggested Mexico as a possible destination. I thought that I might stay there for a while and imagined that he would join me. I had heard nothing from him, however, and I began to think that he had forgotten to reply, or that the letter had been lost. Then just before Christmas, he rang me to tell me he was back in town, and he said that he would think about the trip.

'I'll get back to you, dear,' he said.

Of course, I knew straight away what that word 'dear' meant. That was what he called his mother, and his ageing secretary – the one with the lace-up shoes and the black suits. It seemed that things had altered between us. He had grown cold again, and this coldness was transmitted by the light, dry tone of his voice and through his careful choice of words. Indeed, the addition of that vaguely patronising endearment at the end of the phrase transformed everything and signalled, at least for the moment, the end of our intimacy. As one of Jack's dears, I knew that I no longer represented a lover, nor even a friend. I was, quite simply, another of his middle-aged female acquaintances.

His manner did not surprise me. I had experienced the chill before, and I could guess at his reasons for it: fear that I was becoming too needy, or guilt perhaps; after all it was Christmas, a family time. I was used to his way of dealing with things. There were never arguments or raised voices; we were, I think, incapable of that. He had merely decided, I believe, to allow our friendship to cool a little and frost over for the duration of the snowfall.

On Christmas Eve, I passed by the offices of *Twenty-Eight*. They had been silent for some time and I had decided that it would be prudent to show my face. I did not want them to forget me too. I was dismayed by the greeting I received here however. Only the sub-editor looked up from his desk. Reluctantly, he offered me a cup of lukewarm coffee then, to pass the time, we stood chatting politely about the Christmas gifts he had bought for his wife and children. I left shortly afterwards, but rather than turning back home, I decided to take advantage of the last hour of daylight, and walked up the avenue to the park.

The wind cut through me when I entered the gate, but inside nothing moved and the iced trees were stone still. Walking slowly around the edge of the lake I pondered on the beauty of this silence in the middle of the city. Then I heard a faint cry. I twisted round, but could see nothing in the shadows of the bushes, so I continued along the path towards the boat house and the cafe. Then I heard the cry again, this time closer to me and I peered down at the undergrowth. Hidden in the frosted bracken, I saw a cat. It was silver grey, hardly more than a kitten.

I am not particularly fond of animals. As a child, of course, I always wanted a dog or a cat, but as I grew older, the desire faded. I could not have cared for something that depended upon me totally. But there in the park, under the tree, the kitten was so fragile. It was a pretty thing with shadow grey tiger stripes along its side, a fine Egyptian head and slanting yellow eyes. When it saw me, it stood up and began to rub itself against the coarse bark of a tree trunk. I crouched and reached out to stroke its bony back, but at the touch of my leather glove it slipped away further into the bushes. I called for it gently while holding out my hand, and it came towards me again, sitting shyly just out of reach under the darkness of the tree. We looked at each other.

What would I do if I could pick it up? Would I take it home? I imagined the kitten sitting on the couch or lying on my bed, curled like a cat in a Japanese print, and I stretched out my fingers to stroke him. This time he crept a little closer, hungry I guess, and I caressed his small head, touched his ears and ran my hand along his back. Then noticing that my coat was trailing in the cold mud, I pulled it around me. The sudden movement worried the animal, and he slunk quickly back into the bush. Now I wanted the cat, and like a child I bargained with myself. If I could pick him up and carry him home, I would look after him. If he ran away, I would leave too.

I stretched out my hand and reached for the scruff of the cat's neck. I grabbed warm skin and fur and held it for a second. But he twisted his head sideways and, biting my wrist with his tiny teeth, he managed to loosen himself from my grip. Then I watched as the terrified cat ran off into the dark trees.

That night, instead of going to a party, I stayed at home and opened the box of photographs again. In the autumn, while I was clearing my father's house, I had found nine albums containing large prints that mostly depicted empty landscapes, and thirteen boxes of black and white snapshots from the various holidays we had taken together. The lid of each box had been labelled: *Canoe trip 1928*, *Walking holiday 1930*, *Europe 1933*. Inside the boxes, in nests of curling photographs, were the visual remains of our life together, a kind of diary of my growing up and his ageing.

I laid the contents of *Europe 1933* on the floor and arranged the photographs in chronological order. It was amongst these snapshots that I knew I would find the images I had recalled, the palm trees and the domes of the church.

I was fifteen when my father took me to Europe. I remember that the prospect of this journey injected a certain enthusiasm into his usual dry manner. For several weeks before we sailed he would enter my room almost excitedly with maps in his hands which he insisted we look through together so we could plot our route.

We docked in Naples, of which I can recall very little, then travelled northwards along the Italian coast by train. It was winter time, but the sun was still hot and the sky a sharp blue. From one side of the carriage I could see the plains that spread upwards towards the hills in the distance, and on the other side was the sea. Then, as we turned a corner, the mountains started. There were straight-faced cliffs so high that I couldn't see their tops from the window, and pink stained escarpments dropping down to the water. Puncturing those mountains was a chain of blinding tunnels, linked by five-second fragments of bright villages in a valley or half a minute of olive trees on the cliffs above. It was a frustrating journey, a flickering film flashing black and white all the way to the border.

When we arrived at our destination my father spent most of his time photographing the palaces, churches, and dilapidated fishing harbours. Occasionally he would photograph me too while I would stand as awkward as a young bird – arms lifted slightly away from my body like a pair of immature wings. In one snapshot I am leaning against a rock in a tiny bay that is like a crescent moon of sand. Behind me are palm trees that edge a promenade, and half hidden in their fronds are the blue-green domes of a church. The picture was taken in a seaside town marked right on the margin of the Italian map my father had bought before we left home.

We remained in the town for a week, aimlessly, as if we were waiting for something to happen. He said that for some time he had wanted to return here because my mother and he had visited the town in the early twenties. It must have been a sort of delayed honeymoon. We took rooms in the hotel where they'd stayed, and we climbed up the same hill they had climbed looking for the restaurants in which they had dined. Then we walked along the promenade, under the stone arcades, and down the brown and cream striped pavements that ran past the casino. I carried my coat and scarf over my arm until my muscles ached, it was so hot.

For the Italian holiday my father had brought a small elegant Leica, the strap of which he draped over his shoulder as we climbed upwards through the town. He would always walk on ahead or linger behind in search of those special moments, as he called them. He looked for the shadow of a cloud as it passed across a building, or a thin line of light in the corner of a square. I think he waited for magic, for inanimate objects to come alive, for the sighing of a tree or the sudden cry of a pool of water. In the seaside town he disappeared for hours leaving me sitting on a bench looking at the sea or eating an ice-cream alone outside a café.

On one of those afternoons we walked right out of the town, almost up to the terraces which were covered in low greenhouses that sheltered the winter flowers. My father had long legs and climbed faster than me. I was already hot before we reached the full sunlight and I rested in the shade of a cemetery wall, running my tongue around my dry mouth. He waved at me and came back down the hill with the hotel key dangling in his hand. He told me to go back if I was tired. He asked if I could find my way. I wouldn't get lost?

Afterwards, I stood watching him clambering higher and higher, his camera swinging from its strap. Then he turned off the track onto a narrow path and disappeared out of sight. I was often alone and was used to it, but I remember that, as the distance between my father and myself grew, I experienced, momentarily, a sense of desolation that I had never felt before. It manifested itself as a shortness of breath made worse by the heat and the climb itself. I leant against the wall until he was hidden behind the fold of a hill and when I had recovered, I turned round and walked back into the town.

At the top of the hill, the alleys and the passageways were quiet, drowsy dark ribbon roads where nothing moved. The narrow buildings were sealed, the shutters locked tight across the windows, and the doors were closed. It was only when I reached the market that the road widened and I began to hear sounds – the voices of men and boys. Down there the streets were dirty and the colour of dust. The remnants of last night's dinner lay in the gutter: straggles of pasta and the splayed skin of a tomato were pressed flat into the cracks of the cobbles. I watched a small dog lick at the mess, and when he had finished he ran past me in that sideways loping trot adopted by strays. I slipped down the steps to the town square, my shoes sliding on the greasy stones.

It was at the corner of one avenue and another, just as I was crossing the road, that I noticed I was being followed.

'Hi, Bella,' he said. 'Hi, Beautiful.' He was as rangy as the stray dog, but his skin was tight and brown.

'Hey, Lady.'

I kept my head down and walked more quickly, but I could feel him behind me like a shiver in my back.

'Hey, Bella.'

He followed me all the way, speaking broken English, asking me to stop, to sit down and have a drink with him. He recited the words like song lyrics or a nursery rhyme, without meaning or feeling. I sensed what he wanted, but this was the first time that a boy had ever tried to pick me up. I was acutely embarrassed and vaguely excited. I could feel a spiralling warmth in my stomach, a faint soft beating as he whispered at the back of my neck, but when I looked round, I remember a darkness in his face, a threat.

I said to the boy, 'Go home, go away,' as if he were a dog, and he replied in a hard high voice that I couldn't understand. Then he waved his hand in my face.

I kept walking without looking back, down the shopping streets, beyond the cakes and chocolates, the drying sausages and the dripping hams. I walked to the promenade and the little railway station, past the blank old men who sat outside their doorways. I walked along the striped pavements, by the casino and the crumbling Hotel Paris, until I reached the church with the blue-green domes concealed in the palm leaves. I walked into the porch and pulled open the door. I was sure he wouldn't follow me in there.

It was small: a doll's church with walls the colour of the sea. There were no chairs or pews, so I stood with my back to the entrance looking at the altar that was like a wedding cake: white icing, blue icing, gold piping. The floor was covered in patterned tiles, swaying bands of green and grey, and hanging on the walls were icons – pictures of painted figures against golden backgrounds that were pierced and embossed with stars, moons, or rays of sunlight. I had never seen anything so beautiful, so exotic. I stared for a long time at the warmth of the gold and at the calmness of the blue. The space seemed to cool me.

The Russian Orthodox church was a coda to that strange afternoon. I stayed there some time thinking about my father and the boy, thinking about myself. I suppose that was the moment I began to grow up. The emotions that I had experienced as the boy followed me, and as my father disappeared up the hill, were intimations of adulthood, faint whispers of sexual desire and mortality. Things were never really the same again.

After a week in the Italian seaside town, we travelled north into France. My father had planned to break our journey, and stop at small towns so that we could visit chateaux and cathedrals, but at the railway station in Nice he bought tickets for a train that headed directly towards the capital. He said nothing about his change of mind, although I noticed that he was restless in the railway carriage, fidgeting with his camera, and packing and repacking his small briefcase. I watched him for a while, then I turned away and looked out of the window at the countryside that changed rapidly from yellow-brown peaks to grey-green flatness.

When we arrived in the capital the following morning, I found out that I would not be staying with my father in his hotel. Instead, he explained that he had arranged for me to spend some time with a family who lived in the western suburbs of the city so that I could improve my French. Already slightly dazed by the journey and the changed plans, I did not complain. I realised perhaps that something wasn't quite right and I was sensitive enough not to ask questions.

In the afternoon we took a taxi out of the city, driving along streets that were punctuated by small factories and workshops or scrappy fields where thin ponies grazed. The brick villa in which the family lived was squashed between a river and the railway. It was a large house that seemed to be sinking into the mud. We arrived late – too late for lunch. The table had been cleared by the maid, and the children and their mother were upstairs dozing in their bedrooms. We stood by the window looking out at the mottled afternoon, at the frozen sun falling in spots across the garden. He took my hand, I remember, holding it loosely as if he were embarrassed by it.

'It's only for a week or so,' he said.

He had business to attend to, meetings and paperwork. It would be no fun stuck in a hotel room unable to go out; it was better that I stay with his friends, learn a little French and play with the children. It was all arranged, he said.

After my father left, I paced the bedroom, touching the mirror and leaving a grease stain on the glass. The furniture was brown, the walls papered with dark motifs that sucked in all the light, and outside on the landing, caught in the stairwell, was the odour of decades of chicken and pork dishes laden with cream and butter.

My father was mistaken, however. The children were too young for me to play with. They ignored me, pushing their bedroom door shut as I passed, and their mother, a brittle woman with dry blonde hair, seemed irritated by my presence in her house. I kept away from them all and sat every morning, scarfed and coated, in the strip of garden that ran along the river front. I remember that sometimes Madame would come outside and shake her head at me as if I had done something wrong. Then later, at the lunch table, she would correct my French. Speaking in stabbing phrases and rolling her r's, she challenged me to imitate the sounds that she made. When we had finished eating, after the table was cleared, she bustled round the house, re-doing the maid's work, returning a vase to its proper position on the mantelpiece, running her finger along the edge of the wooden panelling, and checking for dust. She died of cancer some years later, but I think it must have been eating at her even then.

I was much relieved when, a fortnight later, My father and I took the boat to England and then the train to London. Despite the badly-heated hotel rooms, I could at least understand the language, and the food was comfortably bland and plain, no cream or butter. After several days in a hotel near Piccadilly Circus, we went by train to the village where my mother's cousin and her husband lived. They had a large house down one of those deep green mossy English lanes that had once been real countryside. When we arrived, however, urban life was already eroding the fields and the pockets of forest because at the bottom of the garden a mud track had been widened into a road, and beyond, in the meadows, was a string of half-built houses. Sometimes when it wasn't raining or misty, I watched the builders at work on the estate fitting the bay windows, tiling the roofs and smoothing the stucco over the walls.

Vivien's house was old. It had an oak front door and stained glass in the windows of the hallway through which the January light would shine and make patterns on the floorboards. There was a dining room, and a small drawing room with a roll top desk pushed under the window. I remember Vivien sitting there in the mornings writing letters. She was still quite young then. She had short dark hair and wore pink, all the shades from fuchsia to the palest rose. I can remember the colour of her dresses and the fog outside, although whether that was real I do not know. I had been told about the fog before we left home, and I think I may have imagined the sticky yellow veil that descended over the trees and shrubs in the garden.

I arranged the snapshots of Vivien's house, and of France and Italy, in a long line over my apartment floor. I picked them up and examined them one by one, then like a pack of cards I pushed them into a pile and shuffled them, rearranging the photographs into a different configuration.

I thought about my plans for a journey. Europe was calloused and thick with painful layers that I would have to keep on peeling back. Mexico I knew would be smooth like new skin, uncomplicated by memories. If I went to Mexico alone, however, the memory of Jack would still be there, like a ghost, haunting me in the churches and the village squares, and at night in the hotel bedrooms.

I looked at the snapshots in front of me and, as I did so, the pictures I had held in my head for so long began to change. The hot colours were replaced by something more classical, something paler. If I went to Europe I could still write, just as I would have done in Mexico. I could visit cafés and restaurants, describe the perfect omelette, the sweetest apple tart. I could write about the faces of the Italian farmers who owned the olive groves on the hillsides. I could sample a real pizza, one that was made in a Neapolitan back street using strong flavoured ripe tomatoes, basil and buffalo mozzarella.

And there was always the seamstress.

I wanted to disappear too. It would surprise him that I had gone somewhere else because I had something better to do. It would worry him when he picked up the phone and dialled my number only to discover that it didn't ring there any more. He would be anxious when his letters were unanswered and when the door to my apartment remained locked. Eventually he would ask about me at a party and someone would say, 'Oh, didn't you know, she's gone away. I've heard she's quite successful.'

PART 2

She watches the patterns in the wallpaper sliding together and sliding apart like a basket of snakes. Then the curls seem to open and say, 'Drink your milk, dear,' and they push the glass to her lips so that she cannot ask questions. 'Sleep now,' they say, tucking her tightly in the sheets so that she cannot move.

THE NIGHT BLUE SHAWL

I was born sometime between the 16th and 17th of July 1918. My father always maintained that he couldn't be sure exactly what time I had arrived, whether it was just before or just after midnight. On my birth certificate the date is the 17th, but as a child I always believed that my birthday began the day before. From early morning I was excited by the fragrance of the ironed party dress draped over the chair in my bedroom and the smell of baking cakes. In the afternoon there was always a picnic or a trip to the beach. Then on the evening of the sixteenth, after I had washed my face and cleaned my teeth, just before I went to bed, my mother would give me a single present to unwrap. Inside, I would find a small doll or a toy bear or some other soft woodland creature.

Because of the early birthday gift, I could not sleep. I would lie awake looking out from my pillow at the crack between the door and the door frame through which the landing light shone. I would listen to the noises downstairs, the faint hum of my parents' conversation in the dining room, or in my father's study where my mother was wrapping the rest of the presents ready for the following morning. I wish I had realised then that what seemed so ordinary and so comforting – the quiet voices of adults – was a remarkable and temporary phenomenon.

My father was older than my mother. She was only twenty when he married her. There is a small water-colour of her at that age with

73

auburn hair that follows the lines of her round face, but the way I remember her is with a shingle. Her hair was cut so short that they must have shaved the back of her neck: I could feel the bristles on either side of her nape as I put my arms around her when she picked me up. I have no complete picture of my mother, however. I can recall only details: a belt buckle, the flower print on a dress or the knife pleats of a skirt. I can only remember things in close up, not long distance.

When she wasn't there I could still smell her, and I used to follow her scent to the bedroom. I would slip my feet into her shoes, or wrap her white fur stole round me like an embrace. On her dressing table was a drum-shaped music box that I think had once contained powder because when I lifted the lid I could still see the ivory dust clinging to the edges, although the puff must have been lost long ago. If you turned the box over and wound the mechanism with a small key, it played Schumann's *Träumerei*. It is a tune that I have always associated with my mother's absence, a piece I only ever heard when she wasn't there. It was a memory of her, a musical shadow that drifted in the hallway or on the landing or around my bed when I was half asleep.

In the hope that Vivien might tell me more about my mother, I had finally decided to spend a few days in London, before taking the boat to France. When I first began to consider the idea of meeting Vivien, I wasn't certain that we would have much to say to each other or that she would have much to add. Then a Christmas card arrived, long after the New Year: an image of a pair of horses and a carriage driven through the snow by a coachman cloaked in red. Inside the card Vivien wished me a wonderful Christmas and a very Happy New Year and underneath was a short message explaining how sorry she had been about my father's death and suggesting that I should visit her if I came to London. Reading the message as an incitement rather than the polite and vague invitation that it really was, I wrote back immediately asking if I could stay for a few days. I described my route and proposed tentatively that she might wish to travel with me through France and Italy, although as soon as I had put the envelope in the mail box I regretted my suggestion. Her response was slow but positive. How good it would be to meet again after all this time, she wrote. How much there would be to talk about, and what a wonderful idea to travel through Europe, to revisit the places that I had seen as a child. She would have loved to have come with me – how nice to be asked – but she simply had too many commitments at present:

'You know, those little things that always get in the way.'

After the card I was disappointed by her letter. It was gushing and full of the sort of clichéd phrases beloved of unconfident and uninspired writers. The blandness of the words seemed to imply a sense of unease.

Vivien met me at the airport late in the afternoon. As I got off the plane I wondered how I would recognise her, whether some family resemblance would show through after all this time, or whether we would just walk past each other like strangers. But she noticed me straight away, raised her arm and waved her hand briefly. In the taxi, I asked how she had known who I was, and she replied that she hadn't even thought about it, she had just sensed that she was right.

Vivien no longer wore pink but dressed in lilacs and greys and blues. On the first evening she told me that she had stopped wearing pink the day after her husband had died.

'Such a stupid death,' she said lightly. 'It was in the summer, just before the bombs started to fall. He was on leave. He'd gone out with some friends, maybe he'd drunk a little too much, or maybe he didn't see. Those summer nights got so dark. He was running down some steps that led to a basement flat. He tripped and hit his head on the paving stones. He never came round. So silly.' She slid her finger around the edge of her tea cup. 'So un-heroic,' she added with a tight little smile.

75

The Missing

At the end of the second world war, Vivien left the house and moved to a flat in Hammersmith. For the first few months she felt so lost that most days she just sat looking at the view from the window, at the roads that dipped and looped and ended in pinpoints. She was envious, she said, of all these people who were going somewhere in the cars and buses. She saw their faces move towards her, away from her and disappear while she sat immobile. When the sun set and the night grew dark she watched the lights illuminating fragments of road, the ghost grey verges and patches of pavement. She only slept when the traffic was quiet, after the night bus had passed and the taxis had pulled up.

Gradually she forced herself away from the window and tried to read a little. Then she started to knit, but was disappointed by the loose knotted sagging sweaters she constructed. She knew she could never wear them. Finally, as the days lengthened, Vivien realised that she had no choice but to leave the small-roomed flat and drag herself away like a mother relinquishing her child for the first time. Slowly she opened her front door and stepped onto the landing. Then she descended the stairs to the lobby and walked out of the main door to the street. She felt dizzy as she stood looking at her shoes on the pavement, but she steadied herself, and lifted one foot in front of the other, climbing over the cracks. Each day she pushed herself further, learning to walk, trying to find herself.

She wandered for a long time, through the semi-detached roads towards the bed sits and the shabby mews cottages in Barons Court and Earls Court. At first she enjoyed the quietness of the streets, the desolate haunted quality of the empty pavements and the blank windows of the houses, but soon the streets became familiar and repetitive. She discovered that she could not walk far enough to find any differences. The architecture was always the same – the colour of the bricks and the porticoes, even the curtains at the windows, were uniform.

It was the people who changed she said: the taxi driver with the scarred face leaning up against his cab smoking a cigarette, the head-scarfed woman walking her dog, the greengrocer, hands in pockets, standing in the doorway of his shop. Watching them she began to feel at ease again, for even if she didn't talk to them, they were there, each one as ordinary and banal as she.

After several months of aimless walking, Vivien decided that she should apply herself to something more useful. Although she didn't need the money, she began to look work, and finally accepted a post as secretary for a small charity in Grosvenor Square. She soon discovered that there wasn't much to do there either. In the morning she typed a few letters and in the afternoon she folded old clothes and blankets and packaged them up to be sent somewhere. She was uncertain of their destination.

It surprised me that she had never met anyone else. Vivien was in her late fifties and she still looked good. Her skin was taut over her cheekbones and her jaw, she was slim, wore clothes well and her hair was still dark. I wondered why she was alone in that dismal flat, but then there are so many women, chirping women like Vivien, bright and school-girl chatty. And there are others who simply can't connect, who have an ice edge, a hardness. They don't smile enough, or say the right things.

I slept well on my first night in London. Often I find it difficult to sleep in unfamiliar rooms, on mattresses and pillows that don't fit my shape. The bed was comfortable, if a little cold. She had left the window open to air the room and the rain had blown in, dampening the curtains and the carpet by the window so that I had to pull the covers right over my ears.

I didn't wake until after ten and even then I found it difficult to clear my head and adjust to English time. Vivien was waiting for me in the kitchen. When I entered she was standing at the window and looking down at the wide road that went west to Wiltshire and Devon. The room was like the prow of a ship, narrow and rounded at one end with strip metal framed windows, the corners of the glass greyed a little by dirt and age. There was an odd smell in the kitchen, dampness I think, which mingled with stale tea leaves and engine oil that had risen upwards from the road outside. I soon grew used to it.

Although I hadn't mentioned my mother the night before, Vivien immediately began to talk about her at breakfast. It seemed as if she had resolved overnight to tell me everything she remembered, as if she wished to relieve herself of the information that she had concealed for so long.

'You never knew Ashedene,' Vivien said, buttering a slice of bread and then smearing jam across it.

'Ashedene? No, I've seen photographs though.'

'It was so beautiful,' she said. 'The gardens were so beautiful, a shame they had to leave.' She put the knife down on the side of her plate. 'I used to visit when I was a child. Your mother and I used to play in the gardens. There was a weeping willow, we had a sort of den underneath, and we used to make mud pies I remember.' She laughed and wiped the jam from her fingers with a napkin. 'And when we were older, when Edward was about six or seven, your mother used to write plays for us. We had to learn all the words and perform them on the landing, the audience used to sit in the hallway. Your mother used to get so angry with us sometimes because we weren't very good.' Vivien looked up at me. 'I guess that's where you get your writing talent from. Natty used to write such good stories.'

Natty. Ashedene. The old photographs had been pushed into one of the drawers of my mother's dressing table amongst the discarded bottles of hand lotion and face cream. The pictures had never made much sense to me as I had never visited the place; it was demolished before I was born. Ashedene had been designed by my great-grandfather, a house of stone and slate with large windows that gave onto a formal garden of clipped box hedges, lavender and rose bushes, but the photographs in the dressing table drawer did not do justice to the beauty of the place. Whoever had taken them had tilted the camera, partly obscuring the lens with a finger, and in every picture the house and gardens seemed to be sliding down a steep incline towards a dark brown shadow.

All morning Vivien talked about Ashedene and my mother: how Natty would play tricks on the others, how she would put salt in the sugar on the dining table, or fill the decanters with lemonade, and how she liked to snowball fight in the fields beyond the house. Vivien told me that my mother had once wrapped a stone inside a snowball and had thrown it at her brother. He wasn't hurt, but he cried, and she cried, and she refused to play in the snow again. Then Vivien talked about the way my mother laughed. She used to giggle so much that she couldn't breathe and each fit of giggles would end in a red-faced choking cough.

On the second day we took the underground train to the National Gallery and, as we walked from room to room, Vivien told me about Edward who had died of childhood meningitis. Her voice echoed embarrassingly in the hollow spaces.

'He was such a lovely child, like an angel,' she said, staring up at a Raphael. 'It was over so quickly. Thank God.'

She claimed that Edward's death had been the beginning of it all – my mother's slide into depression and my grandfather's problems with the factory.

'That's when they sold Ashedene, that's when it all went wrong.'

We halted in front of a Chardin: a boy in a tricorn hat, constructing a house of cards. I looked up at the boy's face. His lips were pursed slightly while his eyes stared down at the table. In his left hand was a playing card that he held over the construction, anticipating its imminent collapse.

'That's when it all went wrong,' she said again, 'just before the first world war finished, just before your mother got married.' She turned to me. 'You know, your grandfather couldn't bear to stay there. He locked Edward's room, wouldn't let anyone touch it. He would never talk about him after that.'

In the evening we sat in her small sitting room eating bread and greasy cheese from plates on our laps while Vivien plumped out my mother's shadow and made her almost real. 'When they came to Europe that time, when you were just a baby, she looked so well. Her eyes were focused – she looked at things and you knew she really saw them. They were so happy. They showed me photographs of you. How old were you then? Too young to travel, I guess.' Vivien put her plate down on a frail side table which wobbled slightly.

'I had tea in their hotel and your mother gave me a gift that she'd bought in France, a shawl, a silk one. She told me it was hand embroidered. I still have it.'

Before we went to bed Vivien showed me the shawl. She pulled it out from the top shelf of the cupboard where it had been folded for years, the creases fused into the cloth. When she held it up, the light burned through the silk and I could see tiny moth holes that looked like a constellation of stars against a background of deep dull blue. On either end of the shawl were embroidered patterns of flowers entwined around a golden trellis. There were sweet peas and mountain clematis and yellow-tongued honeysuckle that seemed to curl around and up the framework and stretch into the night sky. The colours were still clear – rich reds, yellows and greens.

'Here,' she draped the silk across my arm and I felt it, like the faint brush of a kitten's tail. 'Please, have it, I can't wear it any more, take it, go on.'

In my room I wrapped the shawl in tissue paper and folded it up. It wasn't the sort of thing I could have worn. It was too old fashioned and flamboyant and it would look eccentric draped around my shoulders. But as I shut the silk shawl away in my case, I remembered the seamstress, and I imagined her placing the shawl in its narrow box and passing the package into my mother's gloved hands.

Making supper on the third evening – I think it was Shepherds Pie – Vivien recalled the other trip.

'When was it? Nineteen thirty-three or thirty-four? You were so funny,' she said. 'So skinny and shy.' She laughed and pushed a lock of hair away from her face, 'And now you're so smart, so chic.'

I smoothed the woollen dress over my lap and brushed a few crumbs away. She squashed the potatoes against the side of the saucepan with a fork.

'We had a good time then. Don't you remember?'

I didn't really. There were still gaps in my memory that refused to be replaced by any images.

'Your father was busy. So we took the train and went to the zoo together. Then we had tea. Don't you remember?' she asked again.

Vivien's days were punctuated by tea. Tea was a treat and a respite from tedium, but it was also an event that signified Britishness. Vivien's participation in the making of tea, and the drinking of it, meant that she belonged here in this pigeon-grey city.

Before the war, tea was 'taken' in good hotels. There were sandwiches, Scottish salmon and cucumber and sticky egg mayonnaise, and there was always a glass cake stand piled with pastries, mille-feuilles, and pairs of pink and white meringues held together with whipped cream. But as we sat in the dank tea shop on the last day of my visit, drinking tea as black as tar and sharing a slice of hard crusted cake placed on top of a second-hand doily, she said, 'It's changed so much. It used to be so nice.'

On my final evening with Vivien while we were washing up, she told me things that I had forgotten, or had never known.

'Before she married your father, Natty had another beau, a Canadian. He volunteered as soon as he was old enough, and was killed the first week he was out there. She was heartbroken, just sat on the couch and wept. I don't think I ever saw anyone cry so much. When we took her to the bedroom to lie down, the cushions were still damp with her tears. They never found him. There's no grave. They carved his name on a memorial. It's an arch just covered in names.'

Vivien looked down at the carpet and pushed the toe of her shoe into the pile. I guessed she was thinking of other things then. She shut her eyes for a moment. When she opened them again, she sighed and said how glad she was to be here in her flat with me, just talking.

PIVKIN'S CITY

After I crossed the Channel, the land grew gaping and wide. It is the sort of countryside that one wants to travel through quickly, praying that the train won't stop. There are no trees, hedges or fences, just dull earth under which are buried too many bodies, a countryside of troop movements, refugees and death. Despite its emptiness however, there is something industrial about the landscape. The soil is already worn out through overuse and the plains are cut by a network of roads along which tractors travel, their trailers filled with sugar beet or turnips. I began to wish that I had never come, that I was back in the tiny top floor flat in London drinking tea, or surrounded by the English handkerchief fields I had seen from the window of the train that morning. Why is every journey to an unfamiliar place the same? Why do I always feel dislocated when I pass through colourless landscapes that I can never know?

It was still raining when I reached Pivkin's city. He never called it by its name, it was always 'the city' which added to its magic, I suppose. I had imagined the place as he had described it, a series of story book streets lined with golden palaces and formal gardens, although when I left the station that night, the rain had dampened the pavements and the only residue of anything magical was the reflected light from the lampposts in the puddles.

I had never been here before, or at least I had only passed through. For me, the city was a fractured place reduced to picture book sights that had no geographical connection to one another at all. It was perhaps because of this that I had chosen a hotel far from the tourist quarters, in the last arrondissement, tucked up in the east. I had been told by friends that this was the place to go if you wanted to find the real city. They had said with enthusiasm that this was where the ordinary people lived. The phrase had stuck in my head, and sometimes, during my nights in London, I had imagined those ordinary people. They were plain featured, genderless clones who walked up identical roads, and as they passed, I searched hopelessly for the one face that stood out.

After the dampness of the streets the hotel seemed warm and clean; it was only later that I noticed that the plush and polish was a sham. The parquet under the chairs and tables was thick with dust, and the chaise longue by the entrance was spotted with cigarette burns and wine stains. My room was the same. It had the pretensions of a grand hotel: velvet curtains, monogrammed towels and headed notepaper in the desk drawer, but as I looked more closely I noticed that it was all faded, worn or finger-smudged and torn.

In the days that followed I began to realise that the hotel was simply a microcosm of the city itself. The buildings with their silver roofs and balconies supported by caryatids or fat cupids concealed something grimier and poorer than I had imagined. The mansions were just a front, a thin wall behind which hid long narrow courtyards connecting one boulevard to another. Here was a whole other life, fortressed villages that no one but the inhabitants could penetrate. In this world the washing was strung from building to building, there were chicken coops, kittens that played in the garbage, and lean-to workshops in which furniture was varnished or boots mended.

On that first night in the city, however, I saw only the dust that had gathered in the corners of my room, the tear in the curtain and the stained net that hung against the window. I opened the closet and looked inside, but I didn't unpack. I took what I needed from my suitcase and left it open on the chair, still filled with the folded clothes and shoes. The bed was clean though, and the sheets were well ironed and stretched tight across the mattress.

At first, I slept easily, then I must have woken again, for I heard the sound of the rain against the window and in my half sleep I thought that someone was singing to me.

In the morning I did not want to leave my bed. I had imagined this day for some time and had planned what I would do, yet I could not move. I was rendered immobile by a sort of apathy that had spread over me in the night. It was a sickness that extended from my churning stomach right down to my liquid knees. I lay for a while listening to the muffled voices of the chambermaids in the corridor outside. Then I turned over and looked at the light that shone through the thin red curtains. Now that I was here, the task in front of me appeared insurmountable. The city was too big to grasp.

I reached over, picked up my bag that lay on the night table, and took out a notebook. As I turned the pages, a loose piece of paper that had been trapped by the back cover fluttered onto the bed. It was Pivkin's note: a name and address written in thick pencil and smudged across the ripped page of an old diary. I picked it up and ran my fingers over the paper. It was the first time I had looked at it since I left home.

On a cold day, before I had taken the plane to London, I had met Pivkin in the coffee shop of a large department store not far from my own apartment. I had chosen the location with care. I did not want to take a long trip back to his office and I wished to keep the meeting short. I thought I would feel more comfortable under bright lights and in a space that I knew well.

He was early. I saw him from a distance pacing uneasily among the mannequins and the fashionable ladies. In the artificial light he was uglier than I had remembered and looked like an ageing school boy with his short fringe brushed across his forehead. His hair was the colour of his skin, a flat yellow grey, his nose was snub and his lips slid downwards, further than I had thought possible. We sat at a table in the café and I ordered coffee then told him what I planned to do. Now that I had agreed to meet the seamstress, he seemed jumpier and more nervous than before. His mouth twitched and he drummed his fingers on the table making the cup rattle in its saucer.

'You must be careful not to worry her, not to frighten her, or she might disappear again and we don't want that.' He shook his head. 'No, no, it is sensitive, very sensitive. You must go to Boris Dagarov first. He knows what to do. He will be your contact in the city.' Pivkin tapped the side of his empty cup. 'She is confused sometimes, poor pigeon.'

He seemed to have abandoned the idea of a book or a contract, and simply wished to be paid for the address. We talked money for a short while, but I didn't really care how much it cost. During those icy weeks following my decision to leave I had become used to spending considerable sums on plane tickets, new clothes, and luggage, and the expenditure hardly seemed to diminish the amount in my bank account.

We agreed a price, lower than I had anticipated, and I wrote the cheque quickly and handed it to Pivkin. He glanced at it, then folded it in four and slid it into his top pocket. In exchange he took out a small diary, ripped out a page and across the thin paper, he wrote the address of the library where Dagarov worked. Pivkin passed it to me over the table and I lodged it between the pages of my own notebook.

Lying in my hotel bedroom, I pushed Mikhail Pivkin's note back into my bag along with the map of the city. Then, after slowly washing and dressing, I took the elevator down to the square room where the breakfast plates and coffee bowls were laid. While waiting to be served I took out the address again, unfolded my map and began to search for the road.

The city is a circle through which the river slides like an unhappy mouth. It's as dense as a wasp's nest, a tangled net of thick and thin roads and passages, paths and arcades. I had to put on my glasses to find Dagarov's street, a zigzag line that seemed to change its name several times before it stopped dead behind a railway station. I traced the road with my finger nail, leaving a fine indentation on the surface of the map. My eyes were tired. I rubbed them, then lifted my head trying to focus on the other guests. There was an English family, out of season visitors, and a single man who watched me from the other side of the room. I wished I had taken my glasses off because all I could see was a blurred, jacketed form in the distance.

I looked back at the map, putting one finger on the hotel and the other on Dagarov's road. I could walk there, through the cemetery, down the hill, and along the streets that fed right into the centre of the city. It would take me an hour perhaps. I removed my glasses and put them down next to the bread basket. The man had slipped away, leaving his starched napkin piled like a small mountain beside his coffee bowl.

At the table beside me, the English boy swung his legs, repeatedly hitting the chair leg with the toe of his shoe. He stared at me with his mouth open, airing his tongue which hung loosely over his bottom lip.

'Roger, darling, we don't want to see your tonsils at the breakfast table,' whispered his mother, and the boy slammed his mouth shut. She squeezed a thin smile at me, rolling her pearl necklace nervously between her fingers. When she had turned back to her husband, the boy immediately opened his mouth again and continued to stare. Then he stretched out his tongue as far as it would go and arched it downwards so that the tip touched his chin. I looked back at the map, thinking briefly about Pivkin's embroidery shop, and when I raised my head again, the boy pulled in his tongue, but his eyes were fixed, watching me. The watchful eyes of children are unsettling. What are they searching for? Sometimes I wonder whether I too stare at strangers, scouring them for something familiar, something I have seen in my own face – an expression, a twitch or a nervous butterfly blink.

It was sunny when I reached the cemetery. The puddles from the night before had soaked away into the ground and the gutters were dry. At the top of the hill the paths were ordered in rigid lines, running up and down and side to side within the walls, but as I descended the steps, they began to weave, circling and ending where they had begun. The cemetery was a miniature city. The carved motifs that appeared on the façades of the apartment buildings were here too, repeated on the tombstones and the graves, except inside the walls the cupids became cherubim and the female figures covered their weeping faces with their hands.

Beyond the gates, at the bottom of the hill, the roads were ordinary and the buildings were flat-fronted and grey. Pivkin was wrong; there really was nothing mysterious or unusual about the city. It was simply old and dirty, composed of peeling layers that had been silting up for years. There were layers of paint on the apartment blocks, on the shutters and the shop fronts, layers of mud and cigarette ash ground into the crazy paving tiles on the café floors. And there were layers of torn posters, advertising pre-war *Thé dansant*, music halls and circuses, stuck, one on top of the other, until the paper had stuck together to become thick cardboard. The pedestrians too were swaddled in clothes of pale grey, beige and black, as dull as the buildings and the pavements. They seemed to blend into the city, camouflaged against the walls like moths.

Dagarov's library was on one of these streets but his door was locked. I rang the bell, I knocked, I even called his name, but nothing seemed to move inside. I had not expected this. Libraries were accessible with windows through which one could see the book shelves, and revolving doors that one simply pushed. Dagarov's door worried me; it seemed unreasonable and difficult. I looked around. There was no metal plaque, no card with the opening times, and there was no one to ask. I waited, irritated and frustrated, then slowly, occasionally turning back to look over my shoulder at the door, I walked to a bistro that I had passed earlier and ordered *le plat du jour*. I was not hungry; it was simply something to do. I pushed the boiled meat around the bowl with my fork and dipped the bread into the juice. The waiter took the dish away half full and raised his eyebrows at me.

At two o'clock, I returned to Dagarov's door and tried again. Then I stood on the opposite side of the road to see if anyone entered or left the building, but the street was dead, even quieter than the cemetery. Despite the empty pavements, however, I began to feel conspicuous standing there and imaged that people were watching me from the windows above. I waited uneasily for fifteen minutes, pacing backwards and forwards along the street, then I gave up and wandered away towards the heart of the city.

I walked for hours that day, until blisters began to form on the soles of my feet. I walked right to the other side, just as Pivkin had done. I wandered along the wide streets where the couture houses and the jewellery shops were located, although in the grey afternoon there was something bleak about the avenues and the big squares. Perhaps it was their emptiness or perhaps the light was too flat, but I walked straight past the shops without looking into their windows.

I wandered down towards the river which is fronted by offices and shops and encouraged by a notice that proclaimed '*ici on trouve tout*', I entered a department store. I felt the clothes and sniffed at the perfumes under the domed roof. I even considered purchasing something, and picked a grey fabric belt and a bar of cheap soap, but after looking unsuccessfully for the cash desk I lost interest and returned them to their displays. I left the shop shortly afterwards and walked away, back along the quay and up the hill to the hotel.

I repeated my journey the following morning, through the cemetery, spiralling round the paths. I walked down the streets that I now knew, past the shoe menders and the charcuterie, past *Le Bon Coin* and *La Nouvelle Etoile*. Once again I knocked on Dagarov's door and still it did not open. I thought about Pivkin's story, and his nervousness the last time I had seen him. Then I looked down at the smeared address that I held in my hand. I think I had only ever half believed what he had told me, as I had only ever partly believed Lila and Paula and the Duchess. What stories we tell about ourselves, what fantasies we construct: little lies like embroidered stitches that colour, and curl around the truth.

I ate another *plat du jour* at the same bistro in which I had lunched the previous day, and afterwards I continued to walk through the market to the grand squares. That afternoon I did peer in the windows at the displays of earrings and bracelets on velvet cushions, at the hats tipped over the plaster eyes of the mannequins. And I visited the department store again sniffing at the same perfumes, and pulling out the cheap handkerchiefs and scarves and belts that I had rejected the day before. In a desire for familiarity I had begun to create a routine that I would keep for the rest of my stay in the city, tracing the same streets, lunching in the same café, passing the same shop windows.

With a growing sense of frustration I sent a pneumatic to Dagarov's address. Then towards the end of the afternoon, I sat on a bench overlooking the river, imagining the metal tube containing my message hurtling down the network of pipes that lay in the sewers. I remained by the river for a long time watching the fisherman who had caught nothing all day, and the ladies with their prams walking under the trees. This was the river that would float by the brick villa in the suburbs where I had stayed in the winter of 1933. I looked down at the water and followed the sweet papers and empty cigarette packets that were carried by the current. Then I pictured the objects that floated beneath the surface: the plates and dishes that had been swept in by the floods, and lower still the rusting muskets and knives from the revolution. Finally, right on the bottom of the river bed, I imagined the bloated bodies of those who had disappeared, half buried in the sand: the suicides, the murdered and the victims of war.

The hotel receptionist tightened her lips when she saw me that second evening. It had been raining and I slid off the damp headscarf that I had tied over my hair.

'There was a Monsieur for you. He waited half an hour.' She nodded towards the couch by the entrance, as if I still might see his shadow or the indentation on the cushion where he had sat.

'He left this.' She handed me a card from the pigeonhole that contained my hotel key. It was a visiting card printed in copperplate which read B. S. Dagarov, followed by the library's address. Underneath written in blue ink were the words, *Friday, 3 pm please.*

That night I could not sleep. I looked through my window but the rain had blurred everything: the road, the buildings and the trees. The shadows of the water streamed down the walls, and it seemed to seep through the gap between the window frames. I lay back and thought I could feel the rain drenching my face, sliding along the furrow on my brow. I could feel the drips hitting my eyelashes, trickling down onto my cheeks and falling into the cracks of my mouth. I drank the rain, but it didn't taste good. It fell with such strength that it formed a wet curtain around me. It was so thick that I could see reflections in it. The rain was a mist, a veil, and I began to see things differently.

In the dark, along the side streets, I watched the rain dropping from the balconies, bumping over the stones of the paved passages. On the avenues and the boulevards the angry water arrow-headed down the gutters into the drains. I looked at the people and searched for a face I knew, but the rain had made a flat screen that nothing could penetrate. It made the city a film, a mirage I could not touch.

I walked through the cemetery from the top to the bottom, then along the rue de la Roquette, beyond the shoe menders and the boulangerie to the café on the rue de Charonne. I walked through the Faubourg Saint-Antoine by the courtyards and the dead ends that smell of varnish and paint, and round the sad Bastille to the Seine. I watched the drops disappear into the river and I counted the ripples and the waves. Then, in the sheet of rain I saw a woman looking at me. Her face was thin, and between her eyes was a single furrow. Her hair was wet and the water slid off her eyelashes and down her cheeks and into the cracks of her mouth. She looked at me as if she knew me, and I looked at her because I did know her. I knew her but I could not name her. It was only when she had gone that I realised that the rain had closed around me completely.

BORIS AND IRINA

At three o clock the door was open and from behind it stepped Boris Dagarov.

'Madame, I am sorry for the troubles.' He held out his hand and shook mine; the lightness of his touch was surprising.

Dagarov must have aged badly because his moustache had been bleached grey like an old bottle brush, and pockets of flesh drooped in swags about his face. He wore a trilby hat, scuffed shoes and a badly creased mackintosh that was the colour and texture of brown paper.

'The concierge, she sleep all afternoon,' he said, moving closer. 'She drink too much.' His breath was bad, a mixture of coffee and cheap cigarettes. 'I am sorry you could not be admitted.'

I tried to smile a little, and Dagarov bowed his head gravely. Then he turned and led me through the building to a back door that opened into a courtyard. The yard was long and wide, lined with small workshops: printers, framers and furniture makers. There were broken chairs, tables and narrow pieces of timber stacked against the walls, and on a stool, in the furthest corner, sat a small child holding a string attached to the collar of a black and white cat. The girl watched us, and the cat watched us, twisting their heads as we tripped over the cobbles. Dagarov turned towards her and tried to say something gentle to the child. Then he grinned, showing his yellow teeth, but she remained silent and scowled back.

At the end of the courtyard was a second building with a wide door leading to another hallway and a stone staircase. As I followed him up the stairs, I noticed that Dagarov's hair was raised up on the back of his neck like the coat of an old and angry dog, and that the heels of his shoes were worn down. He seemed stiffer, not as easy or as comfortable as Pivkin had suggested.

We were almost at the top of the building before Dagarov halted. Then, breathing heavily in front of a narrow door on which was pinned a handwritten notice in Russian, he said,

'Library.' He took out a key and unlocked the door.

It was not what I had expected, for there was only one small room. Against the walls were shelves filled with Russian books, and in the centre was a table on which were piled a few magazines in French and English. Dagarov muttered something, picked up the pile and slid them into a rack next to one of the shelves.

'We have not many visitors now, but those we get are badly disordered,' and with his right hand he swept a heap of biscuit crumbs from the table into the palm of his left, and then brushed them carefully into a small teacup containing pencil shavings and torn scraps of paper.

'You're lucky to be surrounded by all these books,' I said, touching the linen spines of those nearest to me. 'You can read them whenever you want.'

But Dagarov looked at me as if he had never even thought of opening their covers.

'I don't have time,' he said. 'I am librarian,' and he turned back to the table and rubbed at an imaginary stain with his handkerchief. It seemed that, for Boris Dagarov, a library was merely a place to keep clean, and the books that it contained were simply oblong objects to be classified and filed but never read.

He continued to dust the table top and the seat of the chair, then he gestured to me saying, 'Come, we meet Madame Dagarov, she make tea.'

At the end of the room was a door even narrower than the first, and an unlit staircase which led upwards to the attic. I had to push my hands against the wall to feel the way. Then, as I reached the last step, the light grew dusky and I saw the silhouette of a woman standing at the top of the stairs with a saucepan in her hand.

'My wife,' said Dagarov wearily as we entered the kitchen. 'Irina Ivanovna.'

She was very short, her hair was the colour of custard and she wore a dress of knitted stripes in turquoise blue and bright parrot green. Dagarov spoke to her quietly in Russian, and she peered at me closely, scrutinising my face with suspicion. I thought for a moment that she was going to reach out and touch my hair, or feel the cloth of my coat, but instead, after having scanned me from head to toe, Irina seemed to lose interest and waddled back towards the sink.

This room was half the size of the library and dark. The skylight was encrusted with a residue of rain and pigeon droppings so thick that the sun could not penetrate. A table had been rammed into the corner under the sloping ceiling, and the bench, on which I was invited to sit, had been pushed next to the wall. There was only one chair, and that Dagarov had claimed by putting his hand on its wooden back as soon as we had entered the room. The table was piled with dishes, clean and dirty, and the edges of everything seemed to be dulled by grease and dust: the skirting and the gas stove and the sink. Even the wall against which I leant felt sticky. Dagarov sat in his chair still wearing his hat and coat as if he were armoured against the filth. He shrank inside the mackintosh, his neck hidden by the collar and his hands hidden in the sleeves. While the library was clearly Dagarov's domain, the kitchen was Irina's.

She made tea, not with a samovar as I had hoped, but with a whistling kettle on the stove just like Vivien's. She poured the black sludge into my cup and added hot water, all the time chirping questions in Russian to which I could not respond. Into Dagarov's cup she added honey and, I think, a little vodka, and then she slid a plate of thin bread and butter onto the table. With her chores complete, she stood wedged between the sink and the table, and looked at us both.

Dagarov sniffed his cup before he put it carefully to his lips. Taking a small sip, he swallowed and then turned to me.

'I thought, Madame, it would be best to speak of the Grand Duchess before I introduce you. She can be difficult.' He sipped his tea more confidently, letting it wash around his mouth. 'And forgetful, she can be very forgetful. She has been through much. But then she was always complicated, a complicated woman, Ania. This is what she call herself now.' He paused. 'She change name like dresses.' He giggled and, unable to prevent himself, he belched violently and the vodka-spiked tea gurgled upwards in his throat. When he had recovered he looked at Irina and said something in Russian. She laughed too, her little fat hand clenched hard over her mouth, before she repeated the words in English.

'Change name like dresses.'

'We help Ania,' said Dagarov. 'We want to help her, she is poor now.'

'Poor now,' echoed Irina.

'We help her to get money,' he said.

'You really think she is the Grand Duchess?' I asked.

'Of course, she is her Imperial Highness, no one else could be that difficult.' Dagarov smirked and Irina clucked like a happy chicken.

'There is no question. Misha Pivkin tell you, I suppose.' Dagarov pushed his teacup away with the tips of his fingers. 'You know, he had been working in mines in Bulgaria and there he heard about Grand Duchess. There was a man there who said he helped her escape, a soldier. He said she was here, hidden in city. So Misha come here.'

'He walked?'

'He took train,' said Dagarov irritably. 'What do you think, walk from Bulgaria?' He looked at Irina and repeated what I had said, and she rolled her eyeballs up towards the blackened skylight.

'He look for her in city. He search for long time, and then he find her in embroidery *atelier*.'

'But how did he know that she was the Grand Duchess?' I enquired cautiously.

'Photograph. Misha tell you about photograph, no?'

I nodded.

'She had jewels, family jewels, but that was stolen by spy.'

'By Kots?'

'Sure,' said Dagarov. 'Kots.' He put his fingers to his moustache and caressed it gently backwards and forwards as if he were soothing a nervous rodent. 'Kots followed her. He watched her all the time. We wanted to help her, so we arrange meeting in restaurant with Grand Duchess and member of her family: a cousin. And the cousin cry and say it was she, and they take her home. Then she disappear. That is what Misha tell you?'

They both looked at me.

'Well, yes,' I hesitated. 'More or less.'

The differences between Dagarov's bare boned account and Pivkin's fat, fleshy tale did not surprise me. Searching for stories was always like that. You dig and sift through the sand until you think you have found fragments of truth, splinters like broken china. You lay them out, scrap by scrap, and you stick them back together again, but sometimes the pieces don't fit, and sometimes you discover holes you can never fill.

'There is one thing,' said Dagarov. He gestured to Irina and she discreetly moved away from the sink into the room behind the kitchen.

'In looking for Ania and in helping her I have spent much of my savings. Misha said he ask you to help me.'

'Help you?'

'You wish to meet her Imperial Highness, then I have to ask you for a little help, money help.' Dagarov got up from his chair and stood looking down at me. For a moment he resembled an uncertain collector of some sort, of tickets, tax, or the weekly insurance dividend. I think he may even have held out his hand.

'I don't have enough money with me right now,' I said quickly. 'I must go to a bank.'

'I see.' Dagarov put his hands into the pockets of his coat and sat down. 'No matter, no matter, when I take you to Ania you can give me then.' He shrank sulkily into his mackintosh again.

From his coat pocket he pulled out a packet of tobacco and started to roll a cigarette on the edge of the table, his white fingers tucking the strands carefully into the roll. He brought the cigarette to his lips and dabbed at the paper with his tongue, and then, without looking up, he shouted something to Irina in the next room. I wondered whether I should leave. I would have liked to have gone. I was tired of their obscuration and hyperbole and I wanted to forget the whole thing right then.

I reached down for my bag, but just as I was sliding my spectacle case back into the side pocket, Dagarov's wife came twittering towards me and beckoned me to follow her into the bedroom.

'*Venez, venez, Madame.*'

It was just as dark in there as in the kitchen, but instead of the grease-lined walls this room was padded with fabric and panels of lace. Some were draped across the ceiling, tent-like, to hide the damp, others were thrown over the wide bed, or heaped on the floor. Irina patted the pile and said something that sounded like, 'Wedding, my wedding,' and then she took my hand and pulled me towards a wall cupboard over which a pair of curtains had been hung. She stood to one side and pulled back the fabric as if she were revealing the stage of the Opéra itself, then clapped her hands and cried, '*Voila, Madame. Voila.*'

The shelves had been removed and replaced by box-like spaces, each one containing an object. There was a school textbook, its corners chewed, a pink hair ribbon that was half singed, a broken saucer, a fragment of embroidered silk, and a squashed *pince-nez*. In front of each object was a cardboard label written in black Russian script.

Irina took down the book and opened its pages.

'Book, book.' She passed it to me and whispered, *'Le petit tsara-vich.'* Then before I had a chance to inspect it, she whisked the book from my hands and opened the first page pointing to a name that I could not read. *'Alexis Nikolaevich,'* she said, putting the book back carefully.

Next she held up the ribbon saying, *'Tatiana Nikolaevna,'* and she looped the satin over my fingers. It was a pitiful object, just a relic of an ordinary life, a dirty scrap that had encircled the hair of a young girl. I held it loosely in my hand while Irina picked up the other objects, giving them names in Russian and, if she knew them, the equivalent in English and in French.

'How did you get them?' I asked.

'Les marchés,' said Irina absently as she turned the *pince-nez* over in her hand.

Dagarov stood in the doorway behind us, the cigarette burning between his fingers.

'My wife collect memorabilia. She find it on market stall in south of city and in north of city. She collect object of Imperial family. She is loyal lady.'

I put the ribbon back on its shelf. All I could think of saying was, 'It's a beautiful collection, very nice.'

'Very nice,' repeated Irina, and then she took out the piece of silk.

'Ania,' she said holding it up to my face and shaking it. 'Ania.' She looked at Dagarov.

'It is sample that she made in embroidery *atelier* – gold bird. Each girl make *apprentissage* work. She learn, she draw picture herself and she stitch it. It is test.'

I looked at the embroidery. It depicted a red bird with gold tail feathers like a peacock, picked out in flat stitch and knot stitch. It was a bird surrounded by a halo of golden flames.

'It's a Phoenix,' I said. 'The Firebird.'

Dagarov nodded and took the silk from me, rubbing it gently between his fingers.

'Why do you think she disappeared?' I asked.

'She is complicated lady,' said Dagarov again. 'She is frightened. She is followed by spy, perhaps. She has been through much, she does not explain, only very little. Sometimes she tell stories but they are not true. You must remember, Madame, she say sometimes things about people that are not true.' And carefully, as if it were very precious, he put the silk bird back into the cupboard.

It was raining again when I left, mad rain lashing upwards from the sidewalks and hitting out at things. I waited at a taxi rank, stranded under my umbrella while the water sprayed my shoes and skirt, and dripped onto my shoulders, soaking into the wool of my coat.

Because of the rain I did not eat that night. Instead I took out my typewriter and set it up on the table by the window. Then I wrote about the courtyard and the child, about the Dagarovs, and their little museum, and about the flea markets, *les brocantes*. When I had finished I pulled the page out of the Remington and discovered that the phrases I had typed were disjointed and unconnected. I screwed up the paper, fed another sheet into the typewriter and began again, differently. This time it was a list.

Post office

Poste restant,

Notice-newspaper

Documents

I lifted my fingers from the keys and listened to the rain hitting the zinc sill. Then I continued again, until at last the words became sentences, joining together for the first time.

'She must have changed her name,' I wrote. 'Changed her name like dresses.'

THE ALBUM

I look at the page now as the sun sets. Typed on the paper is a list that I have centred, one word beneath the other. Below this is the first sentence. It is perhaps the real beginning of the book. Now I start to write again, by hand, across the 90 gram paper that I purchased recently from a small stationers on the avenue Ledru-Rollin. And as I loop the words across the page, I remember that strange place in the city to which I was drawn on the long wet weekend before I met Ania. It was the one place that really fascinated me for it seemed to be an echo of something I had already experienced, a *déjà vu*.

On the day after my visit to Dagarov and Irina, as a way of passing the time, I decided to look at the sights. Slow, slug-like, I followed the text in my Baedeker, reading the columns of history over breakfast like a conscientious child. Then I took a taxi to the cathedral on the river island, although I soon found that the gothic arches and the ribbed vaults held little interest for me. I have always tired quickly when looking at architecture or art. In museums I grow heavy headed and can neither appreciate the beauty of the objects nor marvel at their history. As I wander blindly through the rooms, I merely flick my eyes over the glass cases. I have often been astonished by the speed at which I can move around an exhibition: from entrance to exit in half an hour.

At the weekend, I decided to try something different and took the bus that stopped just outside the hotel to the gardens on the other side of the river. Once there I marched along the lines of Latin labelled evergreens and down the gravel paths, but there was really nothing much to see. Spring was late and many of the flower beds were still empty and the trees were bare. After fifteen minutes or so, I left through the main gateway, and brushed the gravel dust from the heels of my shoes.

I could not find the bus stop for the return journey so I started to make my way towards the north on foot, guessing at the route I had taken earlier. I walked to the river edge and onto the bridge, then I paused, looking at the water that ran underneath. If I were to choose where the beauty of this city lay, I would say that it was right there in the middle of the river. It is only from the river that one can really perceive the city as it curves upstream to the factories, and downstream to the medieval heart on the islands. From the river I really began to believe that it was a golden city.

I leaned against the railings and loosened my grip on the bus ticket that I held in my hand. It fluttered away and dropped into the water. I watched it float, riding the waves for a moment before it spiralled and was sucked down by a small eddy. The river looked inviting; its waves would be as warm as blood as it pushed you gently down towards the soft mud. I leaned further over the railings and, following the current, I watched the pale brown ripples and tiny whirlpools whisking around the pillars of the bridge.

It was the sharp cry of a gull that made me look up. In the clear sky I saw the bird skim over the roofs and then disappear. Once it had gone, I turned towards the railings again, but the river had lost its magic. In just those few seconds, it seemed to have grown cold and unwelcoming. I moved back from the edge and walked quickly away.

It was on the other side of the river, my side of the river, that I found the special place that afternoon. On the right bank, overlooking the bridge and the small gardens that ran along the river's edge, was a large plain building. The ground floor windows had been covered by fine lace, and it was only because someone had propped a broom against the glass, pushing the curtain back like the corner of a dog-eared page, that I could see inside at all. The room was a restaurant, or rather a banqueting hall, for it reminded me of the dining room of some grand school or university. From the ceiling hung brass candelabra, and, arranged in lines, were long tables and benches. These tables were set for a formal dinner. There were glasses for wine and for water, silverware, porcelain plates, and in the centre of each table was an arrangement of pale-petalled flowers, silk I decided, because they had dulled rather than died.

Despite the grandeur of the room and the beauty of the crystal and the porcelain, everything was iced with dust, and strewn between the lights like the finest streamers was a net of cobwebs. I pushed my face against the glass and stared at the scene. It was a lonely place, waiting for guests who were long dead, drowned in the lukewarm river or disappeared. The hall was like the dining room on the *Mary Celeste*, or Miss Haversham's wedding feast. Nothing had spoiled the frosted banquet which was as perfect as the first snow. There were no footprints on the floor and no fingerprints on the plates or the cutlery. I tried the door but it was locked so I squashed my nose against the glass again until my vision clouded.

I thought then of the other empty rooms: my empty apartment filled with furniture. I imagined it like Man Ray's photograph, the dust breeding on the tops of shelves and cupboards, particles reproducing in my absence. Then there were memories of my father's house, the white house on the hill which had been abandoned for six months while he drifted away in the nursing home by the sea.

I had chosen the home for its coastal views. From the garden he could watch the water and the brown yachts on the horizon. I visited him there every fortnight, taking the train and then a taxi to the gates. I rarely returned to the house, only if he asked me to collect something: an item of clothing or a book. Even then I preferred to buy him a new copy of *Washington Square* or *The House of Mirth* instead of opening up the empty rooms and searching along the shelves. I wondered about him when I saw him reading in the garden, licking his dry lips while he enjoyed the unhappiness of Catherine or the downfall of Lily.

He would never read for long, however. As soon as he noticed me standing in the garden, he would put down his book and begin to talk. At every visit he told me something new and with every phrase he uttered I hated him more: his cobalt eyes and his coldness. With each careful word he took another step away from me. When he opened his mouth, I clenched my teeth.

By then he was in his own world for the elderly see and hear things differently. They have lived with the voices in their heads for so long that they believe what they tell themselves and they listen to no one else. Their carapaces harden like the yellow thickening on a toe nail as they shrink into their own thoughts.

Sometimes at the station I would turn back because I couldn't bear the prospect of hearing his thin voice. I would go to a coffee shop and sit there, the guilt beating inside my forehead like a migraine. Eventually, however, I would always crawl back to the platform, catch a later train, and apologise, pleading some excuse. I don't think he minded; in fact I don't think he noticed. When I arrived he would invite me to sit down next to him and we would drink tea or coffee. Then as he talked I would watch the summer flowers curl up in front of me and die.

At the end of September it became too cold to sit outside and his talking ceased, partly because the autumn tired him and partly because the sitting room, where the fire burned in the chimney, was too public for our conversations. We sat there saying nothing, watching the red coals flashing slower and slower until the embers grew grey and turned to ash. On one of those frosted nights, he died sitting upright in his wheelchair. His hands lay neatly in his lap on top of the tartan blanket, his eyes were closed and his mouth shut. There was no drool, no lolling tongue. He did things correctly right up to the end.

Afterwards, I wished I had gone to the house in Bluewood during the summer months when he was still alive. I might have been prepared for the emptiness I felt when I finally opened the front door after the funeral. For the house, just like the restaurant on the river bank, was covered in a dust as fine as grey snow. The objects – the pens and paper on his desk, the cup and saucer in the sink, the unopened letter on the mantelpiece that turned out to be a bill – all reminded me repeatedly that he wasn't there. Then I found a frail white hair that had fallen from his head, trapped in the fibres of a woollen scarf that hung over a hook on the back door. How strange that something as fragile as a single hair is left behind while the body rots inside its grave.

I started to tidy the house, at first concerning myself with the small things only, as if I were rehearsing for the real purge that would take place sometime later. I put the cutlery back in the kitchen drawer, dusted the top of the chest in the hallway, cleaned the cup and saucer in the sink, paid the bill. But it was useless. I realised that the house was too big, the task too enormous, and I spent the rest of the week walking without aim from room to room.

I asked a woman from the town to help me. She had been his house keeper some time ago and I thought that she would be willing to clean and pack. She told me, however, that she had found a new job, and as my father had never really elicited any sympathy from her, it appeared that she felt no compunction to help me in her spare time. So I was left alone, feeling the absence of someone, feeling the absence of two people. Or were they really there in the corners of the rooms, behind the doors, hidden in the smallest places: in my father's scarf, or in my mother's music box that was still on the dressing table in her bedroom?

At the end of the second week I left the house because I thought they were watching me. Yet even as I roamed hopelessly in the garden, kicking the half mouldy apples that had frozen in the heavy frost, I was sure they were spying on me from the upstairs window. In desperation I rang an old school friend whom I knew was unromantic and unafraid of ghosts. She gave me the number of a company who cleared houses and told me in her flat hard voice how to organise two piles – the objects and furniture to be kept, and those to be given away. The rest, she said, I could leave in the house for the men to collect.

I stayed there for four weeks, clearing, sorting and organising, but as I did so, I heard the ghosts mumbling impatiently from the cracks in the skirting and the floorboards, wanting me gone. They were not just the ghosts of the people I knew, there were others too: reproachful unborn babies, miscarriages that had seeped out in the darkened bedrooms, and tearful children who had died of measles and scarlet fever. And there was a suicide, for I am certain that I heard the desperate gulps of a dying man who swung from the rafters in the attic.

Once, I caught sight of my sick mother wearing a nightgown and bedjacket, although she was only a flurry of plain white invalid cloth breezing down the corridor, and I wasn't afraid. But then, one morning soon afterwards, I saw something which really terrified me. I was standing at the bedroom window folding a sheet when I caught sight of a small child in the garden. She slid under the gap in the fence and as she ran down the field to the creek, the birds flew up like loose black smoke above her. I watched the child vanish into a ridge of the hill and, letting the corners of the sheet drop to the floor, I waited for her to reappear. I moved closer to the window and peered out for a time at the empty field, but she stayed hidden. In fact, she didn't reappear until I dreamt about her that night, and just like the dreams I had later in the French hotel, I dreamt of her face and realised that I was looking at myself.

It took me the whole of those four weeks to sort and clear the house. I couldn't decide what to keep and what to give away. I was concerned that later I would regret my choices: after all how could I choose when I was still so angry? Finally, I packed my father's possessions into boxes and left them for the charity ladies from town to take away. My mother's clothes were not so easily disposed of, however. The fur stoles and shawls were all moth-eaten so I burnt them in the garden, but the low-waisted evening gowns and the beaded velvet cloak seemed too good to throw away. I took them out of the closet, laid them on the bed and looked at them from time to time for several days. They were the clothes of a young woman: tiny stitched camisoles, chiffon skirts, lace from Calais, Brussels or Valenciennes, silk from China. They were dresses bought by a husband who loves his wife, or a husband who nets his wife, traps her in the metallic lace of a tea gown and the beaded cage of an evening cloak. In the end I burnt them too. I decided it didn't matter since I couldn't wear them, and she wasn't coming back to get them.

I chose a few pieces of furniture for myself, and the rest I left for the house clearers to remove. The carpets I rolled and tied with lengths of string, then pushed them against the walls. The paintings I took down and stacked. I kept the water-colour of my mother, wrapping it in brown paper and placing it carefully between the skirts and jackets in my suitcase.

The last room I entered was my father's photographic studio. He had set it up after the second world war, buying lights, filters and a long roll of paper, the end of which he had suspended from the ceiling to make a clean white backdrop. By then, however, there was no one left for him to photograph. There was no child or servant whom he could ask to pose in front of his immaculate screen. There were only objects that he placed on tables and lit like still life paintings, *momento mori*. I think by the end of his life his only concerns were formal – composition and chiaroscuro, the droop of a tulip in a glass vase, the shadow of a pear or the highlight on the edge of a silver dish.

Sometimes I used to watch him making things appear in the dark room. It seemed like a trick: the negative slammed into the enlarger and projected four times, eight times, ten times bigger, and his waving hands over the image as he dodged and burned. I remember the red light, the three trays filled with chemicals, and the image materialising from the surface of the wet paper.

I decided to leave the photographic equipment untouched. Whoever cleared the house could unscrew the lights and unhook the paper from the short chains that held it vertical. I did take down the boxes of photographs that he had labelled and dated, however, and I spent a whole day sitting on the floor in the studio looking at them. There were a few images of my father that I must have taken for they were badly focused and the horizon line was slanting, but most of the photographs were of me, squinting at the camera, my face bleached by the sun.

Then I found Sadie – Sadie who always smelt of cake batter, or rosemary and mint – and I picked up the photographs and examined them more closely. There was Sadie in the canoe, Sadie pouring lemonade into a tumbler at a children's picnic by the creek, Sadie tentatively reaching out her hand to touch the muzzle of an ageing cart horse.

I remembered then a distinct moment at a children's party when I was about four years old. My mother had left me at my friend's house and returned home, preferring to wait there until it was time to collect me, rather than helping with the birthday tea or the games of Pass-The-Parcel and Grandmother's Footsteps. As soon as my mother left, I began to cry. I cried all afternoon until my eyes were sore. I cried so much that I must have encouraged some of the other children to wail too. It is the first memory I have of my mother's absence. Maybe it was an intimation of what was to come.

'Darling,' said one of the other mothers to me in exasperation. 'Darling, she'll be coming back at five.'

The lady sat me on her knee and dabbed my eyes with a lavender scented handkerchief and said, to reassure me, 'You know we're here and we love you too.' Then she brushed away the hair that had been stuck to my cheeks with the dried tears. But I didn't believe in her love. I knew it was a temporary expedient. I was incapable of loving anyone but my mother.

Now, I realise that one *can* transfer affection from one's parent to the person who cooks, washes the stockings and the vests, runs the bath and wipes the runny nose. Sadie came to Bluewood when I was seven and at first she frightened me. She was tough, possessing a rural hardness. She was realistic about the chances of the injured animals and birds that I brought home, and unsympathetic towards my childish illnesses. We rarely touched, not even at Christmas or on birthdays, and yet despite this physical distance we were close. I always remember the evenings that we spent together in the warm kitchen. While she cooked or washed up, I would talk about school, and my father, and the ideas that I had about things.

I missed her very much the winter that I went to Europe. I wrote to her every week, sending her postcards which she propped up above the fireplace in her bedroom. When I returned home, she showed them to me, arranged in the order of their arrival. But then, some months later, Sadie and the postcards left the white house. She packed up her aprons, her sewing box and her circular needles, and moved west. She disappeared too, but that was my fault because I forgot her. Someone told me once that the only way to keep people with you is to remember them. Every day you must remember them or they slip away without your ever noticing.

I put Sadie back into the cardboard box marked *Bluewood* and continued to search along the shelves where the negatives had been slipped into paper holders to keep them free from dust and scratches.

On the top shelf under a heap of these sheets, I found a number of blue photograph albums, their pages bound together with golden cords. Most of the albums appeared to be fairly recent; he must have stuck the images into them before his final illness. Maybe he had sat in bed with the squares of double sided tape and the photographs on a tray, organising them meticulously on the pages.

The contents of the albums were dreary, however. They were the usual amateur clichés: close-ups of flowers, the hull of a rotting boat, the wooden frame of the jetty, birds in the sky. But in the last album on the bottom of the pile was something different, a series of pictures that, at first, confused and angered me. The configuration of photographs was unfathomable and I turned the pages backwards and forwards trying to make sense of them. Then slowly, as I looked more closely at the pictures, staring at the blotches and the shadows, I began to understand.

On each left-hand page was a portrait of my mother. The first pages pictured a young woman, not yet married, standing outside houses that I did not know or rowing on rivers that I could not identify. Then followed snapshots of her on their European honeymoon, nameless places that I recognised from my own trip. Finally, at the end of the album were pictures taken in the garden at Bluewood or down by the creek. My mother sat on the swing under the apple tree wearing a wide brimmed hat that covered her eyes, or smiled at the camera as she stood on the same mud islands that I had explored as a child.

Every portrait seemed to have its pendant, for on the right-hand page, shielded by a translucent sheet, was a larger more recent photograph of a building or landscape. These were pictures of places, I decided, where something had happened. They seemed to suggest a loss or a death of some sort.

Then I understood, and the tears came. For every photograph that my father had taken of my mother, years later he had returned to the same location and shot a second photograph. The first portrait in the album showed her as a young woman sitting on a blanket in a field, smoking a cigarette. I could see the line of smoke against the dark band of forest in the distance. Then, on the right-hand page, the landscape had changed, the forest had disappeared, and a wide road had destroyed the meadow where she had once sat.

On another page was an olive tree that grew on a hill above the cemetery in the Italian seaside town. My mother stood beside it, her arm embracing the thin trunk. She wore a pale coloured dress and a silk scarf, the fringed ends of which were blowing gently in the breeze. Next to this image was the same hill and olive tree photographed by my father eleven years later as I ran down those cobbled streets to the Russian church.

At the end of the album was a small snapshot. She seemed older, or maybe the light was bad, for it cast grey shadows under her eyes and her face looked heavy. She was gardening, holding a silver trowel in one hand and a bunch of roots in the other. She did not smile, but rather looked away from the camera towards the creek in the distance. She seemed reluctant to be photographed. Perhaps she thought that, by turning her head and refusing to acknowledge the lens, she would not appear on the negative.

The companion to this picture, the last image in the album, simply showed the empty garden. There was the rockery, a small mound of stones, and a few flowers that pushed through the gaps.

He must have returned to each location, one by one, searching for the exact position where he had taken the original photograph. How he had guessed where to place the camera, I do not know. I suppose he must have measured the distance, counting his strides as he picked his way across the field or up the hill or through the garden. Then he must have set up his tripod, checked the meter reading, focused the lens, and opened the shutter once again.

As my tears fell, I imagined that he had returned to these places in the hope of finding her still there, frozen in the poses that he had photographed ten, twenty or thirty years before. Later, however, I decided that his journeys were a sort of pilgrimage, an act of remembrance provoked by profound loneliness. The photographs spoke of absence and death, but also of continuity. Where she had once been she was no more, but the rockery was still there and the olive tree continued to grow in the mountain soil, and under the highway the roots of the old forest remained buried in the earth.

ANIA'S STREET

A week after my visit to his library, I met Boris Dagarov again, in a café not far from my hotel. It was a large, deserted place, with mint green walls and a mosaic blue floor. Puddles of gritty rain had collected in the grooves between the tiles, and steam crept slowly up the windows. Dagarov was already there, hunched over a table, his long fingers delicately stroking the edge of an ashtray. He looked as if he were floating in the middle of an abandoned aquarium or a drained and derelict swimming pool.

When Dagarov saw me he stood up and shook my hand. He seemed tired and slightly grubbier than before. Under his finger nails were narrow fillets of grime and the lapels of his mackintosh were dotted with grease. Irina is getting to him, I thought. Even in the café I could smell her on him: the odour of overused cooking fat and old dish cloths.

The waiter brought the coffee, slopping it into the saucers as he put it down on the table. Dagarov took out a handkerchief and mopped up the sops, then fumbled with his teaspoon, turning it over between his fingers as if trying to think of something to say.

'Ania is a complicated woman, a very complicated woman.' He looked at me hopefully and I took the roll of money out of my purse and gave it to him. Holding it in his hand, he weighed it for a while then, without counting the notes, he put the wad straight into his coat pocket.

In addition to the money, I had brought a notebook and pen, my Anastasia article, which I had cut out of the magazine, and a camera. I had also folded Vivien's night blue shawl inside a sheet of tissue paper and pushed it into my bag. I was interested in the possibility of coincidences, whether it was conceivable that my own story touched Pivkin's and Ania's, whether the different strands had become entwined in those winter months of 1922. Had Ania rolled the hem of the embroidered shawl and stitched it into place as my parents drifted arm in arm down the tourist roads opposite the Louvre? Had my mother visited the shop that Christmas week and bought the shawl for Vivien? Had she waited while the seamstress packed it into the box, and wrapped the paper and tied the ribbons around it?

When I had finished the dregs in the bottom of the cup, we left the café and climbed up the streets towards Ania's workshop. It was a village of twisting roads, nothing like the city down on the river plain. It was as if the hidden courtyards had been turned inside out. There was garbage scattered on the pavements, and draped over the window sills and rotting balconies was washing, dampened by the rain shower: I felt I was trespassing on the private spaces of the poor. Dagarov walked ahead, padding up the street like an arthritic hound, his hands safely in the pockets of his coat. I could see the shape of his fingers inside his right pocket gently caressing the roll of notes.

Ania's road was as dirty as all the rest. It was a street of small shops: an unlit café, a fruit and vegetable store and a spartan boulangerie, its shelves empty of bread. Dagarov waited for me, leaning against a small shop that had a treadle sewing machine just inside the window. The seamstress's name had been carefully painted in deep red on the glass panel of the door, but someone had scratched away one of the letters and now the sign read: *Mad me Ania. Toutes Retouches.*

'She is here.' Dagarov took his hands out of his pockets and tried the door, but it was locked. While he knocked and called softly, I saw a shadow appear from the depths of the shop. I could see her shape against the light that was shining from the back room. She was short and plump, and her hair was shoulder length, a curling wavy-edged triangle. She rested her hand on the shop counter and I thought I saw the flash of a diamond.

'Ania, let us in,' said Dagarov. 'I have brought someone for you, a friend from Misha. It is important.'

He pointed to me, but the shadow didn't move. Then Dagarov said something in Russian, and the sounds seemed to wake her for she came closer towards the window and shot out two or three words in response. He turned to me.

'Complicated,' Dagarov said, shaking his head. The rain had begun again, dripping from the hems of the shirts and trousers that were hanging over a balcony above him. The water ran down the collar of his coat and Dagarov stepped back into the street.

'Ania, it is raining, let us in please. *Il y a une dame pour vous, une amie.*' He was begging now, for his pride and for the thick wad of money that he clutched in his pocket.

'I will not open the door,' said Ania from inside the shop. 'Go away.'

I saw part of her face, just a sliver of it, as she looked at me. I'm sure she looked at me. I thought that she was silently inciting me to come back later, alone, although I had only seen her lips and her chin; her eyes had been obscured by the back to front words of a street sign mirrored in her window.

She turned away and moved back into the dark of the shop, then the gaunt white face of a kitten appeared at the window and tried to lick at the rain drops.

Boris Dagarov stood on the pavement letting the rain fall on his head and run over his greasy hair. For a moment I thought he was going to apologise, pull the money out of his pocket and give it back to me, but instead he said, 'Complicated, *n'est pas, Madame.* We must

come back when she is in better humour, we can do nothing today.'
He shook his head again. 'Nothing.'

I was not surprised by Ania's refusal to see us. They were like that, the Anastasias, as closed as clam shells. One had to persuade and cajole, wait for the ribbon crack to appear. Only then would they begin to talk. I had already anticipated the difficulty of reaching her in this city of locked doors and concealed streets. I had always known it would take more than Misha's letter and Dagarov's knocking to make her talk to me.

Boris Dagarov continued to apologise as we walked together along the streets to the big square. Then, as he limped down the steps to the metro still clutching the money in his pocket, he promised to meet me the next morning when we would try again. I stood by the entrance until his head disappeared into the underpass, wondering whether to go back to Ania's shop alone, or whether to return to the hotel and write a letter to her explaining who I was. Curiously, I felt encouraged, for I had seen her face and I was beginning to believe in her at last.

JACK

Back in the hotel room, as the sun flared out between the rain clouds, I sketched an idea and made sentences out of my notes. I worked all afternoon while the light fell over the keys of my typewriter. I chipped away at the words, and sculpted the piece. It would be the first in a long series, I decided, notes from abroad, descriptions of the city, the search for the seamstress – but I wouldn't send it to *Twenty-Eight* when it was finished. I would taunt him with the story and try and provoke a nip of envy the only way I knew how.

I called him Jack; to the others he was simply J.P. His full name was printed every month on the first page of *Twenty-Eight*: 'Jackson Powell, Editor' like the 'pow' of a comic book gun, like the first syllable of power. Powell that rhymed with howl. And there was something wild about him, almost lupine: not so much his face, but his leanness, the way he stalked and the way his eyes stared sometimes. He told me once that he liked his name – it suited him, it sounded active and alert. My own name was old fashioned and quaint, he concluded, too innocent and wide eyed.

I first met him at a lunch party organised by one of the regular contributors to the magazine. Jack was seated at the other side of the table, his head half hidden by the wine bottles and the pepper pot, but I noticed him looking. We watched each other in between forkfuls of salmon, and salad that dripped with vinaigrette. I saw brief blinking flashes of his grey eyes, and his brown hair that was swept back from his forehead. The game was furtive and it was exciting seeking each other out stealthily, testing each other.

At the end of the meal I thought he would come to me. I imagined that we might leave together and spend the afternoon somewhere else, but when the guests began to get up and wander outside into the sunshine, he didn't speak to me. Instead he stayed at the table talking with the men while I stood around in the garden listening to the laughter and breathing in the cigarette smoke that floated out of the door. I remember pacing round the lawn, touching the flower heads disappointedly until it was time to go.

I think now that Jack had expected me to introduce myself to him. For when I met him some months later in the offices of *Twenty-Eight*, he mentioned the lunch party and said that he had thought that I didn't like him. I smiled and, denying his accusation, I said dryly that I had been told that he was a very interesting man. It was then, of course, that he invited me to dinner.

Looking back, I think that evening was the best we spent together for we had conversations which required both real talking and real listening. Then towards the end of the evening, while the waiter was clearing the table, Jack said that he liked the way I dressed. He hated bohemian scruffiness which he believed was just an excuse for creases, dirt and unwashed hair. There was a neatness about me that he found attractive, he said. He remembered the fitted dove grey frock that I had worn to the lunch party, and the pale green wool suit in the *Twenty-Eight* offices. He said that I looked beautiful in the black evening dress I was wearing that night with its stiff small armholes and the darts that dug into my chest and hips.

I thought Jack was handsome in a conventional way, except that in someone so clever, so well read, the ordinariness of his beauty was surprising. I had always assumed that an intelligent man should look intelligent, and intelligence meant a fault somewhere: a nose too long, protruding ears or baldness, something of interest, something that bred doubt or uncertainty. Jack had none of that. He said that on several occasions he had been mistaken for Gregory Peck. He was certainly tall enough and had those broad movie star shoulders, but he didn't posses Peck's screen presence or his slowness or gentleness. Jack, I soon discovered, was quick and hard and had a penetrating glare.

After our first night, like a love-sick school girl, I permitted myself to envisage a future. In those early months I was overjoyed to be with him, and a little nervous. I always felt as if I had drunk too much wine when I hadn't touched a glass. I didn't eat much either. I was never hungry then. If I did try to push a spoonful of soup or dessert into my mouth, the food always stuck in my throat.

I found it difficult to part from him after our nights together. When I returned home I thought I had lost something, or left something behind. Often, I would try and turn this uneasy sensation to my advantage, using it as an excuse to contact him outside our usual hours together. Convincing myself that I had forgotten an important book or a manuscript beside his bed, I would call his apartment, but he was seldom there.

When I was alone I would think about him for hours. I would sit at my typewriter without touching a key, imagining his voice, and the way he moved, his long arms and his long legs. Without realising it, I had slipped into a cliché: career girl falls in love with handsome older married man. Yes, I knew he was married, and I knew, or rather was told, that he and his wife had an arrangement. She lived, I believe, in a large house in the country with their daughters while he stayed in his apartment and led his own life. It had been like that for years, apparently. He never talked about his family, although I knew they were there in the background. There was the conventional photograph on his desk, his arm around his wife, and there were pictures sent by his daughters which were invariably pinned to the wall in his office. I must have thought that it didn't matter. I suppose I imagined that he would eventually divorce his wife and marry me.

The Missing

I waited patiently for a year thinking that something might change, that we might live together at least. When Christmas came and went, and nothing had happened, I began to be frustrated with the casualness of our affair. I tried to explain my feelings to him one night, but that was a mistake because it seemed to worry him. He told me not to get too attached, and I remember that he moved away from me in the bed making certain that no part of his body touched mine. The gap between us, the sheets and blankets, gradually grew cold. I didn't hear from him for some time after that. I was being punished, and stupidly I accepted it.

I began to wonder whether there were other women besides me. It was just a suspicion at first, the size of a small hard seed, but it tumbled around in my head, growing larger and larger until it felt like a huge puffy cyst. I was too afraid to ask for the truth. In fact, I think I knew it already, so I gritted my teeth and decided, once again, that it didn't matter. After all, we were such good friends, and our friendship, I believed, would overcome any small jealousy.

'Nothing is perfect,' I said to myself.

About this time, the schoolgirl disappeared and was replaced by what I thought was a mature experienced woman. Jack and I would live separately, I decided, but we would always maintain the rhythm of our relationship: Wednesdays, Fridays and Saturday nights.

It was a long time later, on that May evening, when I really began to understand how silly I looked. I had helped Jack organise the party, inviting the guests, ordering the food and the barman. I even arranged the furniture in his apartment, and placed the little dishes of chocolates and boxes of cocktail cigarettes around the room. I had also bought a dress for the occasion, another tight-armed frock in what I considered to be a sophisticated silver beige, although later I realised that the silk was closer to the colour of mouse fur.

Jack

Jack was pleasant that evening, casually attentive as if I were an acquaintance that he hadn't seen for some time. As the night wore wearily onwards, however, I discovered that I was not the only female to whom he was displaying his charm. By eleven o'clock there was quite a crowd surrounding him, and as I was elbowed away from the group, pushed to its outer limits, I heard someone say behind me, 'Jack has quite a harem now.'

If it hadn't been for Lloyd Harbin and his princess story, I would have left then. I think Jack had arranged it all – the party, the girls and the laughter. He was a strategic, subtly manipulative man. I think he was bored with me, and of course I believed it to be my fault. I imagined it was something to do with my age, the way I looked, my new glasses. So I decided to try harder, make more of an effort, and for a short while I think it worked.

Jack was strangely complimentary about the Anastasia story, saying how good the article was as he flipped through the pages. He was also sympathetic about my father's illness, and once during the summer he offered to drive me to the nursing home. But my suggestion about a Mexican holiday silenced him again, and I didn't hear from him for nearly a month.

On Christmas Eve I went to the offices to distribute Christmas cards and some small gifts for the secretaries. I also carried Jack's present with me, knowing that I would not see him until after the New Year since he usually spent the holiday with his children. I knocked on the door of his office and opened it as I always did. He and his young assistant were standing over the desk looking at proofs. I stood inside the room and Jack looked up. I smiled at him, imagining that he would be surprised and pleased to see me there, but all he said was, 'What?'

It was such a small word, and yet, when he said it, I felt an ice knife plunge into my stomach. The word just snapped out of his mouth, and before I could think of a reply he had turned back to the proofs. I had known the man intimately for almost four years, but there I stood in his office that afternoon, unsure of where to put my hands or my feet, whether to leave or to sit down, whether to be angry or submissive. In the end, I placed the gift on a chair by the door and left.

The next time we talked was in January, just after I had bought the tickets for Europe. We lunched together, but neither of us mentioned our last encounter, nor did I tell him that I was planning to leave. In the weeks that followed, we resumed our affair, although a coldness emanated from him, which I mimicked. I should have known that it was time to tell him that it was over, but I didn't. We lunched and dined regularly again, but we didn't talk or listen to one another. Instead we complained. I irritated him, he said. All the things he had once liked about me now annoyed him. In response, I told him I didn't understand the things he said to me any more, and that he behaved strangely towards me. After that, like children in a playground, we met to taunt and tease. Only very occasionally would we play happily together for a few hours.

I knew that however bad it got, Jack was never going to tell me to go away, just as Jack had never really asked me to come. He had wanted me to introduce myself to him at the luncheon – to make the first move – and four years later he wanted me to remove myself in the same way. It seemed that he wished to remain distant and detached, avoiding responsibility and guilt. He would rather sustain a biting unpleasant relationship than make a definitive move. The sniping nastiness meant nothing to him, just as the romance before had mattered so little.

I remained silent about Europe. It seemed best to disappear. I packed my bags secretly, hiding them in the half-empty closet when he visited the apartment. I asked Lloyd Harbin to deal with any problems or bills when I was gone. He didn't like Jack much, and he seemed pleased that I was getting out. Harbin even came with me to the airport on a bright morning in March. I remember him standing, red-eyed, at the gate, his shirt not quite tucked into his trousers. From a distance he looked like a sleepy, overweight child.

I boarded the plane and watched the city grow smaller and smaller until the wide avenues seemed like the narrow lines on a map. As we rose into the sky, I felt optimistic and strangely liberated, but as we crossed the sea, I found myself wondering what Jack was thinking. I had stood him up for lunch, and I imagined him eating alone, pretending not to care, charming the waitress, and drinking just a little too much. Then I pictured him walking back to the offices, shutting the door, dialling my number and listening to the tone. I wanted to know what he was thinking, whether he was worried about me or whether he thought about me at all. I realised then that it is difficult to vanish, to erase memories and suppress curiosity about what is left behind. It is more difficult than you would think to simply drift away and start again.

PART 3

Nothing she sees is the same as the word she whispers.

From the window, the girl watches the trees. She follows the movement of the leaves in the breeze and says, 'Silk.' She looks down at the light pool on the floor and says, 'Drowning water.' Then she glimpses a knotted lace of hair lying on the wooden boards. It is a dust chain, a frail rolling precious nothing. She picks it up between her fingers and calls it 'daughter'.

She knows that she has lost something or left something behind. Sometimes she sees a group of figures lined up like statues in a city square, but the weather and the moss have eaten them away. Sometimes the figures are like wax dolls that have been left in the sun, or they are ice heads that have melted and disappeared.

THE FILE

I came to the apartment in the summer of 1959 and I have lived here ever since, for almost forty-five years. I can still remember the disappointment I felt when I opened the front door for the first time. I had expected a wide hallway and large bright panelled rooms, but what I found was a dingy corridor, a low-ceilinged sitting room, and a tiny kitchen with a shallow stone sink. I knew, however, that the size of the apartment did not matter at all because I had no furniture and no books, and only one suitcase of clothes. Everything else I owned was on the other side of the Atlantic.

The first items that I purchased for the apartment were a desk and a chair which I placed in the sitting room, and a filing cabinet which I decided to hide in a walk-in closet that they call *le dressing* here. I must have spent several days arranging the documents inside the drawers of the cabinet, because I had accumulated numerous letters, bills, cuttings and stories during the short time I had been in Pivkin's city. I sorted the papers, placing them in cardboard folders, then I hung the folders on the runners. When I had finished, I locked the cabinet and shut the door to the dressing room.

This closet, which is approached by a narrow corridor, the spine of my apartment, is an *impasse*. Consequently, during the years that I have lived here, the dressing room has become the repository for many other objects which I should have thrown away but didn't. As I grow older I find it difficult to be ruthless, to dispose of things that I

127

no longer need. Lodged inside the closet is a broken vacuum cleaner, a pile of old shoes and several cardboard boxes that I believe at some time might be useful. Hanging on the back of the closet door is an expensive hat that I purchased on a whim from a shop on the rue Saint Honoré. It is a little piece of fluff, silk roses and an ostrich feather stuck into a tightly-woven mesh cap. I have never worn it – it doesn't suit me, and when I see it hanging from its peg I wonder how I could have imagined myself as the sort of woman who would wear a pink hat. When I see it I feel a pinch of regret.

At the beginning of last year, just as the weather turned, I finally decided that it was time to return to the closet. I opened the door, and I removed the suitcases and bags that I had pushed against the filing cabinet. I unlocked the bottom drawer and I took everything out – everything, that is, except Ania's notes. I laid the papers on the floor and they spread through the hallway and into the sitting room. There was the Anastasia article which looked and sounded remarkably dated; there was Pivkin's story; and a scrap of paper with Dagarov's address written on it in Pivkin's hand. There was Dagarov's visiting card and there were old bus and metro tickets. Then I found my diaries and notebooks, although these were more muddled than I had remembered and they contained two stories, twisted together like rope. There was even an unfinished letter to Jack that I found folded inside the pages of one of the notebooks.

'Dear Jack, Thinking of me? Wondering where I am? I'm having a fine old time here waiting for inspiration to strike.'

The letter made me laugh but it also embarrassed me after all this time.

I shuffled the papers into piles and organised them chronologically. Then I took them to my desk which I have pushed under the window so that I can see the trees – the only place in this apartment where the thin summer light drops through the leaves. I sat down at the desk and started to make notes of my notes. I started to write again.

The File

I have friends who are surprised that I have not bought a computer, or that I no longer use a typewriter, but I dislike the manner in which the words are beaten from the machine, the way one has to hammer the keys, numbing the tips of one's fingers. I prefer to write by hand, using plain white paper and a fountain pen. I find that the phrases come smoothly, at the same pace as my slow thoughts, although gripping the pen is painful now. It has taken me eleven months to get this far.

Last night I knew it was time to look for Ania's file again. I remember that I had slid my notes inside the covers of a grey folder which I had pushed to the back of the cabinet. After so many years, I was afraid that I wouldn't find the folder again, regardless of my careful filing. I was worried that it might have slid down behind the drawers or turned to dust in the intervening years. I even wondered whether it existed at all, for occasionally I believed that my memories of Ania were false, that I had invented her shop and the days that I had spent talking to her.

But the notes were still there, although the pages were creased and the ink on the paper had faded somewhat. I took the folder to the armchair by the fireplace, and read each page slowly. The writing was flat as if I were describing a photograph or a painting, something imagined rather than something real. I wasn't surprised that I had abandoned the article.

According to my notes, Dagarov and I went back to the shop twice, but Ania wasn't there. The shop shutters had been pulled right down to the ground and they were padlocked. After the second visit, I decided to write her a letter; I still have the carbon copy. I explained who I was, where I came from and why I was interested in her. I told her much more than I should have done, but I received no reply.

Despite her silence, I decided to trail across the city and visit the landmarks in Pivkin's tale. One afternoon, I took the metro to the

Russian Orthodox church and travelled along a route that runs for twelve kilometres, crossing the north from east to west. Part of the track is elevated, carried on iron columns over the canal and the railway. From here you can look down at the barges and the tops of the trains, or into the second and third floor windows of the apartment blocks that face onto the track. After the canal, the metro line tips south towards the bourgeois city with its desolate avenues that are punctuated by parks, squares and bronze statues of triumphant statesmen. It is here that the Russian Orthodox church is located, standing like a theatrical backdrop to a short but imposing road. I entered the courtyard and looked up at the mosaic panel and the tiny golden domes that crowned the towers. Then I saw the steps that led to the entrance where the seamstress had blown her nose. That afternoon there was a small group of tourists who stood there waiting for the doors to be unlocked at three o'clock. I joined them and inspected a board in the porch where fragments of paper had been pinned. They were handwritten notices in Russian and, as I ran my eyes over the cyrillic script, I wondered whether they were the pleas of desperate families hunting for lost relatives.

Inside the church, the walls were dark, old gold, cracked and burnished. There were icons hanging on the walls and candles burning in the alcoves. Wandering around vacantly, I stared at the images, although the light was so poor it was difficult to see anything. I was disappointed, for despite its grandeur, the interior had none of the clarity of my Russian church. I didn't stay long and as I strolled away, I realised I could recall nothing of the church apart from a foggy cloud pierced here and there by candle flames.

I walked for an hour clutching my map, hoping eventually to find some trace of the embroidery shop. I passed beyond the department stores and the grand hotels to the Opéra, and then through the maze of covered arcades that link boulevard to boulevard. The *quartier* was not as smart as Mikhail Pivkin had suggested. There were only a couple of small shops, and a few restaurants and cafés that fed the business men who worked in the Bourse and the banks. I turned off a wide boulevard into the smoke-black street that Pivkin had named, but found no trace of the shop, no shadow of a sign, no flakes of pale blue paint on the façade. In its place stood a laundry that serviced the restaurants by washing away the lunchtime stains from the tablecloths and napkins. I waited a while by the doorway and thought about Kots. I looked at the ground where he must have stood and at the graze marks on the pavement that had been formed by the bottom of the door, then I squinted through the window. The staircase at the back of the shop, which had once wound up to the *atelier*, had been removed and where the counter had once stood were piles of clean pressed table linen.

As I write this, I check my notes from time to time and I am frustrated by the vagueness of my writing and the lack of accurate dates. I know that my journey to the church and the shop were undertaken in one warm afternoon. I know that, as I dined that evening, I began to consider the possibility of moving out of my hotel room and taking an apartment. In my notebook I have written two addresses of potential accommodation that I may or may not have contacted. I also know that it was at this time that I bought that foolish pink hat. I had noticed it on my journey between the church and the embroidery shop, and I must have returned the following day to purchase it.

But how long did I wait before trying to contact Ania again? How many days passed before I took the bus up to the grimy village on the hill?

ANIA

I do know that the sun was shining the day that I met Ania, because I wore my spring trench coat and a light woollen dress. I know that the shops on her road were closed – it must have been a Monday – but that her shutters were pulled right up and the door was open. And I know that, this time, the seamstress sat at the sewing machine pushing the wheel and directing the fabric underneath the needle.

I stood in the doorway and watched her work. Ania's hair was as red as a squirrel's coat, and her fingers were thick with rings. She moved briskly, coaxing the thick velvet through the machine. Then, when the seam was finished, she looked up.

'Excuse me, you wish information?'

'My name is Frances Daye,' I said. 'I wrote you a letter. Did you get it?'

I was a little frightened of her then. I was worried that she would come close and snap at me with her bad teeth. She looked nothing like the others. She possessed none of the sadness of Paula, nor the mock regality of the Duchess. Her face was round and there was a slight droop of flesh below her jaw, but her skin was smooth. It was a girl's skin, undistorted by experience and pain, or maybe her tears had simply worn the creases away.

She smiled briefly as she released the fabric from the sewing machine.

'I got the letter,' she spoke in English. 'I suppose they tell you that I'm the Grand Duchess Anastasia?' She grinned, stretching her mouth into a long wide line. Then she snipped at a thread hanging from the fabric with a pair of tiny scissors.

'Misha is a sentimental fool and Dagarov is a liar.' She flicked away the loose fragments of cloth from her jacket. 'So you want to interview me, for your paper. You want to make a little money out of me like the fool and the liar.' She paused. 'So what are you going to write about?' Then Ania laughed – a short dry mocking laugh that came from the back of her throat.

I didn't reply. I opened my mouth but no sound emerged.

'What does it matter anyway? It was so long ago.' She sighed deeply and looked at me for what seemed like a long time.

'Maybe we have coffee, seeing you have come all this way for nothing.' She took off her glasses and folded the heavy curtains that she had been sewing. 'Yes, we have coffee,' said Ania decisively. 'Please sit.' She pointed to a chair covered in cat's hairs and disappeared into the back room.

I looked around. There was a high counter behind which were shelves filled with fabric and reels of coloured thread, and in one corner of the room was an old mannequin, whose proportions – bust, waist and hips – had been adjusted outwards as far as they would go. I sat in the chair and began to pick the white kitten hairs out of the patterned pile of the upholstery.

'I have coffee and cake,' said Ania, carrying a metal tray. 'It is not good cake, it is disgusting cake, but it is all there is. I buy it from cheap shop.' She shrugged her shoulders.

She had a husky voice that ran up and down the scales as she spoke. She had bright brown eyes, or perhaps they were blue because they seemed to change in the light. She was colourful, dressed in a green jacket, an orange skirt, and a fuchsia scarf tied around her neck. She wore an amethyst broach on her lapel, jade earrings and a turquoise bracelet. Her lips and nails were painted coral and her eyelids sea grey. I wondered where Pivkin's sorrowful seamstress had gone.

'I knew you would come back,' she said, settling down into the chair beside the sewing machine. 'I knew you would come back without him.' She poured the coffee. 'Go on,' she said teasingly, 'go on, ask me a question, Mrs Journalist.'

'So if you're not the Grand Duchess, who are you?' I drank the coffee which was strong and looked at her over the edge of my cup. Her eyes were direct. She stared at me confidently.

"I'm Ania, that's all.'

'Why do you keep changing your name?'

'Why not?' she replied. 'Anyway it is not safe being Russian, even here.'

'What are you afraid of?'

'What are all *émigrés* afraid of? Watching eyes, listening ears, people who come to your house asking questions.' She laughed again and this time it came from her solid little belly.

'Why do Pivkin and Dagarov think you are the Grand Duchess then?'

'Ah, Misha, he is a romantic, he wants to believe. He would say that any young Russian girl was a Grand Duchess. He used to tire me so much then, always whispering over my shoulder when I was working, always telling me how hard life was for him, always breathing down my neck. And then one day he thinks that I am Anastasia. Me!' She lifted up her hands and gestured to her face. 'How is it possible? I laugh at him. I tell him don't be stupid. I say, leave me alone, fool. But then he goes and tells Dagarov and that is mistake. All Dagarov sees is money. He likes money and he likes order. He likes things in their right place. In the *atelier* he used to line things up in rows with the best silk on the top shelf and the cotton lining on the bottom. You understand. Dagarov is cheat, dirty liar. He is always bothering me. I never let him in.' She cut the cake into quarters and into eighths and then handed me a slice.

'You see the film, the one with that Swede woman? What's her name?'

'You mean Ingrid Bergman?'

'Yes, Bergman. It was like that film. There was always Misha whispering round me, telling me to do this and to do that. He wanted the money you see, but there is no money. I knew that. There is no Russian jewels. It all went with the war. I tell him to stop but he never do.'

'And that's why you disappeared?'

'I didn't disappear. I left. I went because I am not the Grand Duchess. Misha say over and over but I am not. I want him to leave me alone so I go away. I take the train and I go to another town in the south. I work in a factory making slippers. That's all.'

'And what about Kots?'

Ania seemed to shrink a little. She put down her cup and looked at me doubtfully like a cat who doesn't trust the hand that strokes it.

'Why should I tell you anything? You'll tell the whole world in your paper.' She pouted briefly and then flashed a smile that was like a rapid streak across her face. 'You like the cake, disgusting, no? Dry as sand.'

'The cake's good,' I lied as the crumbs stuck in my throat.

'And what about you, Mrs Journalist?'

'Miss,' I corrected her.

'You've come all this way just for me. I am flattered, but you've come for other things, no? Maybe I interview you?'

I thought it was best to play her game for a while so I told her about the magazine, about my writing, about Vivien and the trip to London. I even mentioned Jack. Then I told her that I had been to the church and the embroidery shop. She said that she couldn't even remember the name of the street and that she certainly would never be able to find it again. She paused for a while.

'I liked working at the shop before Misha messed it up.' She smiled again. 'You have finished?' She took the cup from my hands and put it back down on the tray. 'You come back if you want. You ask me questions and then I ask you questions,' she giggled, 'and we have conversation. We have coffee and bad cake again. You like that?'

The following day I returned and showed her the blue shawl. I took it out of my bag, unwrapped it from its tissue paper and laid it on my lap. She seemed delighted. She picked it up, holding it closely to her eyes.

"It's so long since I have seen these things. They are beautiful. Such beautiful things we made.' She stroked the silk, letting her fingers pass over the stitches. 'You see,' she pointed to the bouquets of flowers growing up the trellis. 'They are shaded. We call that needle painting. You take the thread and make little stitches to fill the petals, but you have to keep changing the colour of the thread from light to dark, that's why they look so real. Each flower has a glass bead at the centre, like the centre of a real flower, but the trellis is flat and it's just one colour. In the scarf there are things that are real and things that aren't. You see?' She handed it back to me. 'I only sewed the seams. I used to roll the hems or stitch the linings. Only sometimes did they let me embroider. I was good. I had good eyes then.'

She watched me touch the shawl. 'You should wear it.'

I could see that Ania was running her eyes over my grey suit. I had bought it from Barneys just before I left home and I was pleased with it. There was a sheen to the cloth and the cut was sharp and tight.

'You choose such dull things,' she said. 'You are so. . .' she searched for a word, looking around the shop as if she might find it there. 'You are so prim,' she said finally with a little flourish. Then she rose from her chair, took the shawl and looped it round my neck.

'That's better. . . more. . . more interesting. Come.'

She made me stand up and walk to the dust-specked mirror that hung on the wall close to the counter. 'You see?'

I saw a small-boned, thin-faced woman in her early forties. There were the beginnings of short faint pleats above her top lip and around her eyes, and there was a deep frown line between her eyebrows. Her hair was light brown and her eyes were hazel.

'No, no, not your face,' said Ania. 'Look at the scarf, look how it changes the suit.'

I looked at my neck that was partly covered by the silk, and I looked at the silver wool of my jacket. Ania stood behind me adjusting the shawl so that the flowers would show. Maybe it was the reflection of the gold embroidery thread or the glass beads that lightened my face and wiped out those lines I had just seen.

On my next visit to Ania, I wore the shawl. The weather had changed and I chose a light green dress, fitted at the waist and pencil slim round the hips. I draped the shawl around my shoulders and I fastened it with a pin that had belonged to my grandmother. Ania smiled when she saw me. She had warmed a little, I think. She seemed less obstructive and less challenging.

'Where do you come from, Ania?' I asked as we drank coffee.

This time I had brought a gâteau: thin layers of sponge filled with a light strawberry mousse and topped by a translucent, shiny red currant glaze. She had slid the cake onto a plate and was now cutting it carefully into narrow slices, but the filling was forced out under the pressure of the blunt knife.

'From the Black Sea,' she said, without looking at me.

'The Crimea. Your family came from the Crimea?'

'Yes, from the Crimea.' She had divided the cake into portions and was delicately placing one of them on a cracked saucer.

'And what happened to your family? Where are they now?'

She licked her fingers that were smudged with pink cream. 'That's good, a good cake.'

'What happened to your family, Ania?' I asked again.

138

She handed me the saucer, took a slice of cake for herself and then started to dig a teaspoon into it. 'I left them behind. I went away. I had to.' She put the cake into her mouth and chewed slowly. 'This is really good. You will bring me another next time, Frances?'

'Why did you leave them behind?'

She put down her saucer. 'I was married to a man. He looked after me, but I was ill and it was hard for him.'

Ania picked up her saucer again. She took another mouthful of cake and swallowed. 'I went away. I could not stay. And anyway it was getting bad then, the situation, you know?'

'You left your husband?'

'Yes, I left him. He wasn't sorry. I think he had met someone else. It happened a lot then.'

'And what did you do? Where did you go?'

She had finished her slice of cake. 'Frances, I cannot remember everything. I don't know why you want to know. You can't write that in your paper. Who cares anyway.' She waved her teaspoon in the air. 'I am not the Grand Duchess.' Then she eyed the rest of the cake, which was balanced on the edge of the table next to the sewing machine. 'I think I have another slice. And you?'

Every time that I visited, I brought her a gâteau from the patisserie that was on the opposite side of the square from my hotel. It was a light clean shop and the cakes of the day were laid out on a deep sloping shelf in the window. I would choose a cherry cream Fôret Noire, a slick black Opéra, or a Saint Honoré with clusters of iced choux pastry filled with vanilla custard. When I returned to Ania's shop in the afternoon, I would carry the sagging box containing the new gâteau, and Ania would rush to the back of the shop and find the only plate large enough to take it. She always pretended that it was a great surprise despite the fact that she had asked me the day before to bring her a new cake. She would untie the ribbons that had been knotted round the box and wrap them around her neck or her wrist. Then she would undo the cardboard latch and peep inside like a small child.

'This looks really good,' she would say. 'We try it?' and carefully she would transfer the cake from its greasy chocolate or raspberry smeared cardboard to the plate, all the time sucking the tips of her dry fingers.

In my notes, the cakes are indelibly linked to the different questions I asked her. On the afternoon that I brought the square regal chocolate cake, I enquired about the photograph of the four sisters and their father. Did she remember it? Did she still possess it? I asked.

'There is no photograph,' she replied, a handful of black cake crumbs halfway to her lips. 'I don't know what you talk about.'

The following day I bought a Rum Baba, its centre filled with fruit and cream. As she was finishing her second portion, I asked, 'Ania, how do you know that the Russian royal family has no money or jewels hidden in a vault?'

'Only idiots think that there was money, 'she replied. 'It is a well-known fact that it was all used up,' and she shovelled the remains of the rum-soaked sponge into her mouth.

'How is it that you speak so many languages, Ania?' I inquired the day that I purchased the praline-filled Paris-Brest.

'I study hard. I am a good student.'

Then a week later, as she was lifting the citron tart from its box, I pointed to her neck and asked, 'Where did the scars come from?'

'Sometimes, Frances, I think you are not polite,' she replied. Then cutting the tart into fours, she broke off a piece and slipped it between her lips. 'It was childhood accident. It was a train accident,' but she couldn't continue. Her mouth was filled with a lemon filling so rich that it glued her tongue to her palate.

The cakes appeared to have a cumulative effect. With each visit, Ania became easier, more accustomed to my questions and more willing to answer them. It was a custard mille feuille that encouraged her memories of the *atelier*, and a simple fruit tart that induced her to talk about Kots. It was a raspberry tart in a sweet pastry case spiked with almonds. The thin layer of cream had been flavoured with amaretto and the fruit had been dusted with sugar. The pastry, I remember, was particularly sweet, and the raspberries particularly succulent.

'Who was Kots?' I asked.

'My lover,' she replied simply, spitting crumbs over the skirt of my grey suit.

THE SEAMSTRESS'S STORY

Ania could not recall where she had first seen the boy.

Perhaps it was in the waiting room of a railway station because she remembered a line of benches that stretched into the distance and a clock on the wall that said midnight. Although she was certain that the room had swayed. There was a gentle rocking sensation that surely signified the movement of a boat through waves or a train slowly clattering along the tracks. Or maybe it was she who pitched from side to side with her arms wrapped around her body. In any case, she said, it was dark outside, and there was no landscape, or sea, nor even a railway platform. There was nothing at all.

She had sat opposite the boy for hours until his pale head had become a fixture: his thin light hair and his mouth were so familiar that he was almost a friend. She called him a boy although he was probably older than she was. He was one of those people who retain until death a certain childlike freshness of face and an easy amiable spirit. She also noticed a shyness in his eyes when he looked at her, which wasn't often, for most of the time he sketched or wrote on the thick grainy pages of a notebook.

'What are you drawing?' she asked casually, suffering none of the discomfort or awkwardness that she might have felt had he been a stranger.

The boy lifted his head and looked to see where the voice had come from. Then he smiled.

'The dog.' He said, pointing to a puppy she had not noticed, curled up, his bottom sliding on the tiled floor as he tried to push his paw into his ear to scratch it. The boy leaned forwards and held his book so that she could see, but she could only make out a few faint lines in the darkness.

'Why are you drawing the dog?'

'Because he's there and because I like dogs.' He turned the pages of the book indicating the rapid sketches of the restless puppy. She shifted on the bench, but still she couldn't see them clearly enough.

'I like all animals,' he said, handing her the book. He was encouraged by her questions and heartened that someone was taking an interest.

On the earlier pages were realistic pencil sketches and water-colours of beetles, butterflies and moths. These she understood, but they were followed by bizarre cubic shapes of wild animals: a blue deer, a yellow wolf, a black fox set in a red and green forest. She squinted at the images.

'Don't you draw anything else?'

'No,' he frowned. 'Nothing else is worth drawing. The animals are the most important things, the truest things.'

'Why are they blue when they should be brown?' She pointed to the deer. 'Why are they so jagged?'

'Because I try to make them as real as possible, real for me. To make something real doesn't mean making it look the way you see it. It means making it look the way you feel it or how you think it feels from the inside.' He watched her anxiously. 'Does that make sense?'

'I think so,' she said, looking back through the pages to the wolf and the green horses.

'You see, the lines and colours have a meaning too,' he continued. 'They should make you feel something. It's not just the subject that's important, but also the way in which it is drawn.'

She only half understood, but the sound of his voice was pleasant, and she nodded.

'I like them,' she said. 'Do you only make small paintings?'

He took the book from her hands and closed it.

'At home I used to paint on canvas but I had to leave them all behind. Now I can only make sketches. I have an idea for a large painting though, something really big.' He put the book back into his bag. 'But it's only an idea.'

'Why did you leave?' she asked.

'Because of the killing,' he paused. 'It's been like that all my life. My father was killed before the war, my brother during the war and my mother afterwards. There's no one left. I don't want to stay. I don't think the new country will be any good either. They promise it will be better for people like me, but I don't believe them. I just want to be left alone to think what I like.' He buckled the straps round his bag and looked up at her. 'Where are you going?'

'To my family,' she replied. The words came straight out, as if she had learnt them by heart. 'But I don't know whether I will find them, or whether they will want me.'

She tried to appear unconcerned by straightening her dress and attempting to push out the creases that had formed on her lap.

'What will you do if you can't find them?'

'I don't know.' She shrugged her shoulders.

He looked at her for a long time, as if he were assessing her. 'Can you sew?' he finally asked.

'Of course. I learnt when I was small.'

'Take this.' Out of his jacket pocket he pulled a business card. It was scented, sandalwood she thought, and printed on the card was a man's name and an address.

'That's the *atelier*,' he said. 'They promised me a job as a draughtsman. They employ needlewomen too.' He looked up at the clock. 'I have to go now, but maybe you could think about it.'

He started to walk away but she called out, 'What's your name?'

He turned, 'Yakov. Yakov Kots. And yours?'

She thought of something quickly. 'Anna,' she replied.

She was alone now in the vacuum, feeling the space around her, feeling for the strings that held her down, and connected her to the others. But when she stretched out her fingers she touched only one thin thread, as fine as silk and as invisible as a cobweb.

In the morning she didn't take the train. She had always feared the moment of finding her family again. Probably they had forgotten her by now or assumed that she was dead. It had been so long. And she was no longer sure that she wanted to return and take up the life she had lived before, whatever that was.

'Too many things change,' she said to herself.

Then she thought about the boy. He was a friend, the only person to whom she had talked for weeks. Amid the strange vagueness of the world she inhabited, he seemed solid and tangible.

'Why lose touch with the only thing that seems real?' she whispered.

Before she arrived at the door of the *atelier* she invented a past. She had adjusted her face to look like a lady's maid or a dressmaker, and she had pulled her collar over the scars. But it was simpler than she had imagined, as simple as sewing the French seam and the button-hole on a plain piece of white cloth. When she had finished, the work mistress inspected the stitches and then looked at the girl's hands. 'What happened here?' she asked, touching a finger that was crooked and gnarled.

'I was a novice in a covent, the soldiers came. . .' Madame nodded sadly, letting the girl's hands drop gently back into her lap. Then the woman sat back in her chair and opened one of the drawers of her desk. Taking out a folded linen smock and a cap, she said, 'You will start work this afternoon at two o'clock.'

The Seamstress's Story

The seamstress was taken upstairs to the attic where she was shown her bed and told to rest before lunch. But she could not sleep. All morning she lay there, hoping to hear the boy's voice from the floor below. Then, at lunch, she lifted her head and ran her eyes along the faces at the table. There were redheads, brunettes, blondes, a whole garden of girls, like open-faced marigolds, wilting lilies and tight-petalled roses – but the boy wasn't there. For amongst all the flowers there were only scarecrows: a dwarf with a miserable looking dog by his side, an old man who sucked his teeth, and a beer-bellied pantomime villain with hair so black that it must have been dyed.

All week she slid from hope to despair. She listened for the boy, holding her breath at every sound. Sometimes she was certain that she heard him on the other side of the door, or on the floor below, but he never emerged from the office or climbed up the stairs from the shop. By the sixth day she felt the cobweb line between them weaken, and on the seventh night as she lay in bed, the girl was sure she felt it snap. With her eyes shut tight, she pictured the future she had imagined, and like a building in an earthquake it began to shake and crumble, and her hopes fell like roof tiles, timbers and stone. In her vision, she stood before the pile waiting for the dust to settle, knowing she would have to find something else to hold on to: the scarves and the shawls that she hemmed perhaps. At least she could touch them. At least *they* were real.

On the eighth day she sank down into dullness, a tedium of neatly-stitched buttonholes, bindings, backstitch, and openwork seams. She felt as flat as the cloth that she worked: the matt blue silk clasped in the embroidery frame, and the plain cotton lining spread out over the table. On the ninth, tenth and eleventh day, the girl just sewed, watching the needle advancing painfully along the seam or the thread loop then stretch over the cloth as she pulled it tight. She repeated the action again and again, ensuring that each stitch was of equal length and of equal distance from the last.

But on the twelfth day, after she had given up all hope, he appeared: a pale face sitting at the supper table, smiling timidly as he asked one of the needlewomen to pass the bread. He didn't see the girl who sat in the shadow. She didn't see him. She didn't even lift her head. It was only when she began to clear the table, as she walked around and took the boy's dish, that she realised who he was. She felt a silent explosion that shuddered right up to the top of her head and all the way down to the backs of her knees. He seemed pleased to see her too because he held out his hand to touch her own, but then they both pulled back quickly, sensing that someone's eyes were upon them. And all he said was, 'Thank you,' as she carried away the bowl and spoon.

It took days of muffled conversations for the seamstress to comprehend what had happened. The boy had been promised the post of assistant to Andrei Nicolaevich. He was to help create a new range of beaded dresses and evening jackets, and would design the sea scenes, forests and flower gardens that were to cover the crêpe de chine.

'But you have no sense of form,' sniffed the designer, flicking through the pages of the sketch books.

'Naive, badly drawn,' he wailed, waving his hand in the air as he dismissed one sketch after another.

'No good. Simply no good.' Andrei Nicolaevich slid from his desk towards his couch and reclined. Then he dabbed with a handkerchief at the perfumed perspiration that had settled on his brow.

'Leave me,' he whispered as if all his energy had been sapped. 'Leave me. Just go.'

It was Madame Hortense who had offered the boy the job of doorman, a replacement for tooth-sucking Raoul who had developed rheumatism in his legs.

'That is all I can do for you,' she had said.

The boy had refused the offer at first and had resolved to look elsewhere for work. He tried jewellers, wallpaper manufactures, carpet weavers and architects, but all of them had looked at him, looked at his book and turned him down. After two weeks, he had no choice but to return to the shop and accept Madame's proposal.

'It's not so bad,' he whispered to the seamstress in the evening when she wiped the table of bread crumbs. 'At least I have time to think.'

During shop hours the boy's task was merely to open the door to customers, but at the end of the day he delivered packages and parcels to the apartments and hotels of rich clients. It gave him time to see the city, he said. 'It really isn't so bad.'

When the evenings grew light, the needlewomen were permitted to wander down to the river or up to the boulevards, as long as they went in pairs or small groups and returned before Dandy locked the doors at ten. No one noticed that the seamstress slipped out alone, and no one really cared. She would linger in the attic room until the others had left, then grab her coat and her hat and hurry down the road as if she were trying to catch them up. In the arcaded square, she would creep in and out of the arches, looking at the windows of the small shops, all the time watching in case she was being followed. As soon as she was certain that she was really alone, the girl would whisk out of the square, turn down a dark side street and run along the avenue that led to the Tuileries gardens. There she would wait for the tall uniformed boy who had just disposed of the parcels of gloves and slippers at the back doors of the Hotel Ritz or the Bristol.

During the summer and the low-lit evenings of the autumn, they wandered down the narrow alleys side by side, saying nothing. They didn't need to talk. They merely drifted quietly and comfortably together under the trees. The silence was good, she thought, although there were times, when the sun was warm or if they sat close to each other on one of the benches, when she wished that he would take her hand or just utter a few soft words. But it wasn't until winter that the boy began to talk, and then he talked only of Dagarov.

The Missing

It seemed that Boris Dagarov believed that the basement was his dominion. He considered that he possessed certain privileges: powers over those who slept there and rights to every object stored under the beds of his companions. Rights, the boy said, that Dagarov exercised regularly, by stealing a bottle of Dandy's wine or borrowing a pair of clean socks that belonged to the boy. Dandy and Yakov tolerated his behaviour simply because they knew that their lives were easier that way. They neither talked about the arrangement to each other, nor complained of it to anyone else. All through the summer they had silently accepted it, but as the sun disappeared and the skies grew leaden grey, the real disputes began.

The boy had been sitting at the table in the basement painting a golden rabbit. His sketches were no longer drawn from life. The animals had become mythical creatures or hybrids: horses with lions' paws, cats with the split hooves of goats. They ranged over the pages, coloured in subtle water-colour tones of red, blue and yellow. That evening he was carefully brushing an ochre wash across the paper when Dagarov snatched up the sketch book. He examined the pages closely and sneered at the pictures. His lip curled and his moustache twitched as he rifled through the book. Then holding it up, open at a double page of blue bears and rose pink unicorns, he called to Dandy. 'Hey, the boy's blind or an imbecile, I can't work out which.' Laughing, Dagarov threw the book down upon the table.

The following evening, the boy returned to the basement carrying a wooden chest and a padlock. He locked all his belongings inside the box and he kept the tiny key in the top pocket of his uniform.

Realising that he could no longer help himself to the boy's possessions, Dagarov grew irritable and short-tempered. He snapped at every opportunity, nagged or made fun. He hated the boy's remoteness, his wispy sensitivity, his tentative smiles and his quiet voice. At supper that night, Dagarov taunted him by calling him a moron and a ninny, but it was later in the basement when the real trouble began.

As Dagarov slouched in his chair smoking a cigarette, and the boy lay reading on his bed, a small mouse squeezed out of one of the holes in the skirting and crept towards the table at which Dagarov sat. It was a young mouse, too young to know fear, for it seemed to run quite happily from chair leg to chair leg. The boy turned his head slowly and held his breath. He was fascinated by the velvet ears that curled on the creature's head, and by the tail that looked like grey silk thread. He watched the mouse's snuffling curiosity, and its pleasure in adventure. Then he smiled at its delight in the discovery of a strand of tobacco that had dropped into a crack between the floorboards.

It must have been the silence that made Dagarov look round. Perhaps he no longer heard the boy's breathing or the turning of pages for he looked towards the bed and saw the boy's face and his focused eyes. He followed the boy's gaze right down to the floor beside his own feet where the baby mouse crouched with the tobacco delicately balanced between its two front paws. Then without saying one word, Boris Dagarov lifted his foot encased in its heavy boot and smashed it straight down on the animal.

Looking up, he saw the boy's astounded face, and he laughed. He laughed so violently that he made the water pipes rattle and the light bulb swing. The boy stared back at Dagarov's grotesque face, and he smelt the foul stench that belched from the pits and crevices of the store room manager's open mouth. Then the boy looked down at the corpse of the flattened animal, and he felt something harden in his heart.

It was a well-known fact among the needlewomen that Dagarov smuggled out of the *atelier* off-cuts and remnants of expensive silks and brocades which then found their way onto the market stall of a man called Phillippe. They were only very small remnants, useless for anything but handkerchieves and, in all truth, had they remained in the store room they would have been given to the girls or thrown away. Instead, thanks to Dagarov and Phillippe, the cloth enriched the lives of the poor women in the east of the city. The off-cuts were cleverly transformed into collars and bindings which hid the frayed edges of coats and jackets. Or they were used to cover buttons, or turned into patchwork to make party frocks for their children. The only problem was that the money earned through these transactions went straight into the deep pockets of Dagarov's coat: coins and notes that were later surreptitiously transferred to a small cash box stashed beneath a length of velvet on the top shelf of the store room.

So who followed Dagarov that winter afternoon as he left the *atelier* with the brown paper package under his arm? Who peered through the window of the café and saw the exchange? Who followed him back, and watched as the roll of notes was placed carefully in the cash box?

Was it Vera, the buck-toothed bitter girl to whom Dagarov had promised a necklace if she opened her mouth and kissed him? She had done this willingly, pressed up against the wall of the store room with her eyes closed, all the time imagining the apricot cameo dangling in the crease between her breasts. She could see it clearly – the links of the gold chain and the pale carved shell – as Dagarov's teeth banged against her own. After three weeks of waiting, however, Vera's neck was still bare.

Was it Dandy, who was tiring of Dagarov's complaints about his dog's night-time flatulence, and the comments about flea bites? Surely Dandy would have no scruples about informing on Dagarov, or black mailing him for a few centimes.

Or was it the boy who should have been delivering a box of slippers that day to the proprietor of a rotting palace near the Bastille? He would have gladly seen Dagarov punished or dismissed. Did he continue his journey beyond the palace, through the courtyards and up the narrow paths? Was it the boy who crept along the streets in the shadow of the creased brown mackintosh?

Whoever followed Boris Dagarov on that Sunday afternoon told Madame, and on Monday morning at eight thirty precisely, the store room manager was summoned to her office. The door was shut behind him, but the girls could still hear the words from Dagarov's loud mouth, streaming out from the gaps between the door jamb and the wall. They heard him deny the accusation and they saw him vigorously shaking his head. But Madame pushed on with the snippets of evidence: the store room ledger in which the missing cloth had been recorded, the name of the café where the deals took place, the metal cash box still wrapped in its heavy velvet. Dagarov begged. Then his begging turned to blustering anger as he realised that someone had spied on him.

'Who was it? Who sneaked?' he cried, while Madame sat tight-mouthed and silent.

'It must have been the boy,' shouted Dagarov, sharply. 'It was the boy, wasn't it?'

But when the seamstress asked Yakov about the incident that evening, he swore that he knew nothing. He said that he had returned directly from the Bastille, caught a bus back up the rue St Antoine, past the town hall to the Louvre. He said that he had watched the well-dressed tourists walking by the palace and the wealthy Parisians carrying home their boxes of cakes for tea.

'It wasn't me,' he said to the girl.

Misha Pivkin appeared two weeks after Christmas. He was a small man with a flat face that was as yellow and as pitted as a round of cheese. He was introduced to the staff as Dagarov's assistant, but the girls maintained that he had been appointed to keep an eye on the store room: after all there was little else for him to do. Misha followed Dagarov everywhere, treading on his heels, getting in the way. In the store room, like a nurse assisting a doctor, he would stand beside Dagarov and hand him a needle, or a button, or a pair of scissors to cut a length of cloth. For most of the time, however, Misha Pivkin would simply sit at the store room table and stare dreamily at the girls.

He was captivated by the needlewomen, by the way they spoke and the way they moved. He adored them in all their forms, fat and thin, pale and dark. As he looked out of the store room on that world of swaying hips and delicate wrist bones, at the hint of a lace camisole against a fleshy bosom, at the blonde strands that escaped from a cap, he believed that he could love them all. By the end of his second week, however, after having carefully assessed each needlewoman, he had settled on one girl alone.

Despite the beauties of Kiev and Vladivostok, St Petersburg and Odessa, it was the taciturn seamstress in the corner with her smock fastened right up to her neck who captured Misha's colourless goggle eyes. Perhaps it was her modesty, or the intensity with which she worked that attracted him. Or perhaps it was because she was the only girl who never looked his way.

Misha dreamed about her day and night, and as his confidence grew he began to whisper gently in her ears. If Madame's back was turned, he would shuffle softly towards the girl and release a moist hissing monologue towards the back of her damaged neck. She would shiver and try and brush the damp words away, but he was always just behind her muttering about a walk in the park or an afternoon on the river.

Sometimes at supper he would sit next to her, and then in the evenings he would follow her to the Tuileries, and down the paths beside the river. His tenacity was a disaster for the girl. She could no longer keep her rendezvous beneath the plane trees and was forced into

154

long winding diversions, while making cautious signals to Yakov who stood bewildered in the distance. They gave up on the gardens. They decided that it was no longer safe, and after a number of complicated and devious experiments wandering along streets they did not know, the seamstress and the boy finally settled on the Russian Orthodox church. It was dark and empty inside, and there were alcoves and shadows.

Every day Misha tried to seduce the girl, and as the weather grew warmer so did his words. They became so unbearable they made her squirm. She twisted her fingers inside the cloth that she sewed, and curled her toes inside her shoes, but there was nothing she could do to prevent him from sidling towards her in his tartan slippers. She was an easy target. All through June he carried on, insinuating, fawning, cringing, and by the middle of July the seamstress could take no more. Following an invitation to a dance on the quay that night she started to sob, gently at first, and then more rapidly, and with the sobs came tears that she had held back for weeks.

'Just leave me alone,' she said to Misha. 'Just go away.'

Even when he inched back into the store room, her sobs did not cease. They were like hiccups, deep spasms that rose up from her chest. Then the tears ran down her cheeks, and her neck, and the skirt of her dress. She wept long into the next day until her lungs and her throat ached, and her nose turned purple. Madame rubbed a pomade on her forehead and dabbed her face with water, and she was given tea, coffee and brandy, but she could drink none of it.

At the end of the second day the seamstress had grown so fatigued that her weeping eased. While the needlewomen swept the floor of threads, fabric and tears, the intervals between her sobs lengthened and at supper she began to take a little food. She dipped her spoon into the soup, crumbled the bread onto her plate and after swallowing a few mouthfuls she was allowed to leave the shop alone. The needlewomen, worn out by the weeping, were glad to see her go.

The Missing

The seamstress walked towards the church. She ran her hand along the stone of the buildings as she passed and felt the roughness graze her fingers. When she reached the steps, she could see the boy inside the church leaning up against a dark wall, the bands of gold on his uniform illuminated in the candlelight. She walked towards him and whispered to him, which wasn't easy for her words were forced out by the sobs. To comfort the girl he put his arm around her shoulders, and smelt the residue of the milky soap that she had used to wash her face. The intimacy surprised them both. They had never been so close. She could see the mole on his left cheek and the short smile lines that bracketed his mouth. As she noticed all this, he bent towards her and kissed her on the lips.

This was the first time that the girl had been kissed, a kiss provoked by love not by lust. This was the first time that she had noticed the softness of another person's face and the deepness of his mouth, and the warmth of his fingers on her neck. They kissed, and kissed again. They kissed until they heard footsteps on the gravel in the courtyard outside. Then they drew back, and the girl raised her hand and stroked the contour of the boy's face, following the curve from his eyebrow right down to his chin. She smiled gently at him, and then without saying a word, she turned away and wandered out onto the steps.

It was almost night now and the balconies and window boxes were shades of grey, but in the dull streets the girl could see colour: the reds and blues that the boy had painted in his sketch book, and the gold flashes of his uniform. She stood breathing clearly for the first time in two days and, taking her handkerchief out of the pocket of her skirt, she blew her nose for the last time. Then she ran down the steps, out of the courtyard, and back to the attic room.

Things changed. The kiss provoked an edgy restlessness in the boy. During the day he paced up and down outside the shop rubbing the gold buttons clean on the sleeves of his uniform. In the evening he put his arm round the girl's waist, and he held her tight against him while he talked of leaving the *atelier*. He was impatient to start again, he said. He wanted a better job and an apartment big enough for them both.

Unlike the boy, the seamstress slipped down into a dream. For her, the kiss had been enough, and the memories of it lulled her sleepily towards inaction. Her sewing was completed in a haze while the needlewomen were merely vaporous forms and Madame was just a sharp voice in the distance that faded in and out of her consciousness. There was only one thing that the girl's drowsy eyes noticed on those late summer days. Misha Pivkin had begun to behave oddly. He watched her differently, as if he were judging her, or measuring her like an object.

In the autumn Misha finally approached the seamstress again. This time his voice was flatter, less insistent, and his eyes were hidden by a dim grey shadow.

'Have you seen this?' he asked, pointing to a newspaper where photographs of Anastasia and the Duchess had been printed side by side. 'She's a fake, isn't she?' And without waiting for the seamstress to reply, he said, 'This is you. *You* are Anastasia!' And he held up the photograph of the Grand Duchess.

'You must be mad,' she said, laughing out loud.

Misha, offended by her response, waved his finger at her.

'Why deny it? I have proof, Mademoiselle, I have proof.'

Of course, he never presented the proof, and initially the boy and the seamstress thought it was just a high flown scheme. They concluded that Pivkin was looking for a girl who dimly resembled the Grand Duchess Anastasia, a girl whom he could parade like a fairground attraction in front of reporters, photographers and gullible minor aristocracy. The two decided that Pivkin had no intention of taking it further by restoring the girl to her royal grandmother or her aunts. They were certain that Misha merely considered the scheme a quick way of earning a little cash in backhanders from the newspapers, and a means of procuring invitations to dine from the rich *émigrés* of Paris.

As the days cooled, however, it seemed that Misha was more serious than they had at first thought. Each time that Madame Hortense was out of the room, he would hurry to the girl with a scrap book of photographs in his hand which he would pass in front of her.

'Don't you remember this?' Misha would implore. 'And this, and this. . .'

All she could do was shut her eyes and shake her head.

Later, when he had returned to the store room, the girl was certain that she saw Misha present the book to Dagarov. The store room manager turned the pages with one hand and thoughtfully twisted the end of his moustache with the other.

'I think Misha has said something to Dagarov,' the seamstress told the boy in the brown gloom of the church that evening. It was cold now and the scarf that she had wrapped around her neck was thin. She shivered.

'I don't trust Dagarov,' the boy replied. 'He hides behind doors and listens to what we say. He's as slippery as an old trout. I wouldn't be surprised if he worked for them.' The boy waved his young hand vaguely towards the east.

At night his dreams of the seamstress changed to nightmares where the girl was reduced to the size of a mouse. He would see Dagarov's white hand clutching at her, and his long polished nails tearing her skirt as he dragged her along the tracks of a railway line. The boy flew at the man, prising fingers away from fabric, levering them up one by one. Then he took a knife and slashed at them, cutting the fingers off at the junction where they joined the man's palm, but the stumps grew back, sprouting like bean shoots that encircled her neck, her waist and her narrow ankles. The boy bit at Dagarov with his teeth, gouging out chunks of flesh along his arms and neck and on his face. Then he caught hold of the moustache and ripped it away leaving a bloody gash that was filled with a nest of curling worms.

The boy's dreams were brightly coloured and lucid. They resonated long into the day. He felt Dagarov looming like a rain cloud, and Misha lurking like a shadow. It was time to go, he thought. Marching from one end of the shop front to the other, a network of plans unfolded in his head as he looked down at the fissures and cracks in the pavement. But he was fearful that even in the labyrinth of the city, Misha or Dagarov's grasping hand would catch the girl. It was time to go somewhere else.

Two days later the boy handed the girl a train ticket.

'Meet me at midnight and bring your things,' he said. 'Make sure they don't see you leave.'

That night the boy and the seamstress walked to the station, and next morning they took the first train south.

ANNETTE AND YANN

The town was just one street, edged at its southern limits by a grey stone chateau set on a mound of earth above the river. From the town, the building was a mass of turrets and fortified walls that had been hurriedly erected by anxious knights or wealthy lords who wished to show their power. The chateau was empty now. It had been abandoned by the family, who could no longer stand the leaking roofs and the ivy that thrust itself through the gaps in the shuttered windows.

At the other end, at the northern border of the town, was a white flat-roofed factory, as long and as horizontal as the chateau was tall. It was a modern palace of efficiency, a place of conveyor belts and vast rooms of jabbing sewing machines and vats of glue. The factory was clean, clinical and well maintained. No flower had been allowed to push its roots down into the soil around it, and if any plant dared to shoot it was pulled up as soon as a leaf appeared.

The factory and the chateau were like two bookends that supported between them a row of small shops. There was the charcuterie, the bank, the drapers, the café and the boulangerie. The street could have been modelled on any one of those avenues in the outer arrondissements of the city, except that in the city there were narrow roads behind, criss-crossing down to the next boulevard. Here there was nothing. The town was merely a narrow façade of civilisation beyond which were hidden damp vegetable plots and fields.

The Missing

It took only fifteen minutes to promenade along the street from factory to chateau, and on Sunday afternoons that was just what the town's people did, aimlessly trudging towards the river.

Annette and Yann took two rooms over the charcuterie where the smells of paté and ham, which they could not afford, rose upwards from the shop. But the fragrance of boiled and roasted meat mattered only on a Sunday morning, for the rest of the time Annette punched her needle downwards through the tartan cloth and Yann sat on the production line packing slippers into boxes.

He smiled when he first saw the slippers. They were like those that Misha Pivkin wore as he shuffled from the *atelier* to the basement. He laughed as he imagined Misha lifting the slippers from the tissue paper and placing them gently on his toeless feet.

In the workshop, Annette was fascinated by the fabric she sewed. As she pierced the tartan with her needle, the intersecting lines of muted colour that traversed the cloth seemed to hold pictures for her. In the dark green squares she saw a fat old man in a chair, a rug over his legs, and a woman by his side who called him Bertie.

After the third week, however, when the laughter and the fascination had dispersed, both Yann and Annette learnt to follow the nodding rhythm of the sewing machines and the sliding pace of the conveyor belt. Then, on Sunday afternoons, they too wandered, with everyone else, aimlessly up the street towards the chateau.

The first year passed quickly, as did the second, the third and the fourth. Eight years passed before Annette began to realise that nothing would change. They would continue in the same way until they died: intervals of work broken only by Christmas and a summer fortnight when they took take the train to the seaside. The phrase 'time flies' is so true, she thought, placing the cover on her machine at the close of another dead week. Time was fluttering away from her, and all she could do was to run behind trying to catch it up.

She hated the countryside and the way that the town fizzled out untidily into the fields of red cows or stunted vines. She missed the glamour of the city and the beauty of the objects she had made. She missed them badly, and the sensation was like a sore on her body that would never heal. If she tried to ignore it, something would always rub against the wound and open it again, and then a discharge of frustration and disappointment would seep out.

Yann seemed happy though. In the first year he had discovered that the kitchen of their apartment was wide enough for a canvas to be hung on the wall, and large enough for a small table to be pushed beside it to hold his paints and brushes. He began to work again, nervously dabbing the paint onto the surface in short timid strokes. The initial painting was a disaster, however. For a whole day he looked at the mess. The green impasto dashes and the flat red glaze stared out sorrowfully, and he was sure he heard the blue-black lines laughing at him.

'Can't do it, can you?' they muttered, as he took a cloth drenched in turpentine and wiped them all away.

The second and the third attempt were just as bad, but the fourth layer of paint seemed to promise something. He decided that there were patches towards the bottom of the canvas that had begun to work, and in the evening he pointed them out to Annette. In the gas light she saw a jungle of animals that leapt and played, and in the centre floated Annette and Yann arm in arm and covered in what looked like flower petals.

'It's beautiful,' she said, although this time she wasn't sure that she meant it, and to cover her lie she turned back to the sink to rinse the teacups.

She was surprised, however, when a week later she found him pulling the canvas off the frame and then stretching another length of fabric in its place.

'What was wrong with that?' she asked, looking at the crumpled painting on the floor.

'It wasn't right,' he replied. 'It wasn't coming together.'

For eight years in that small kitchen, Yann worked on the same scene, painting and repainting the same canvas, and when the weave was worn out, he would stretch new cloth over the ageing oil stained wooden frame.

Annette was jealous of Yann's obliviousness to everything. Wrapped in his own animal world, he didn't see, as she saw, the ticking hands of the clock that relentlessly turned round and round, or the changing pages of the calendar that hung from a piece of string on a nail by the kitchen door. He didn't even see that his hair was thinning on the crown of his head, or that his shirts were frayed at the cuffs and collars.

In her lowest moments Annette wondered about his paranoia in the city and his fear of Dagarov. He is always running away, she thought, and she was angry that they had come to the town for nothing. Now, she was certain that he wouldn't leave. He seemed happy in the security of repetition: the stretching and priming of the canvas, the mixing of the same colours and the reiteration of the same motifs.

At last, in the summer of the ninth year, Yann noticed her finger nails chewed down in boredom and the sharpness of her voice. He took her torn cracked fingers in his hand and asked her what was wrong. She told him that, more than anything, she wished to return to the city. She told him that in the early evenings, after work, when she was supposed to buy the bread for supper, she would run down the road to the *presse* and flick through the magazines on the shelves. She would look at the pictures of the models posed in front of misty drapes, wearing gold silk that slid over their shoulders and their hips. They were a whisper of something more alluring, more lovely, more subtle than the earth-faced peasants whom she passed on her walks out of town. Then she told Yann that she dreamed of taking a skilled job again where she could make tiny hand stitches in satin instead of the clumsy coarse-threaded seams she produced in the slipper factory.

Yann listened to Annette and asked her for one more year. He said that he needed one more year to finish the painting. He needed time to correct the composition and the colour, and then it would be right, he promised.

She began crossing out the days in pencil on the calendar. And slowly, in anticipation of the move, she started to pack away the china and glass, which they rarely used. To distract her, Yann brought her a kitten, a gentle cat who kept her claws hidden in their sleeves of fur. They called her Blanche although she was a tabby, and they treated her like a small child, feeding her at the table, and laughing at her spiralled nest in the bedclothes.

Blanche learnt to play with a cotton reel. She danced on her back legs and sometimes she would respond to Annette's questions in a throaty rumble. As she grew older, she would follow them on their Sunday afternoon walks down the street towards the river and the chateau. Blanche was added to the painting, portrayed as a long-necked cat who wound herself around Annette's flower-clad legs. The cat's eyes were a lick of winter blue, her coat a ripple of orange and black. She was the best bit of the painting, declared Yann, standing back from his work.

On the coldest day of the tenth year, Blanche vanished. She didn't return for her night time dish of milk, or the scraps of beef fat that Annette had placed in a bowl on the kitchen table. They called out of the window. Then they climbed down the stairs and went onto the street, but Blanche wasn't there. The following day, Yann pulled on his boots and hat and searched through the gardens at the back of the houses. The snow blew round his ears and the ice numbed his fingers as he peered into barns and pig styes. Annette asked the neighbours who showed a vacant-eyed lack of interest in the whereabouts of the cat. No one, amongst all the people in the hard muddy town, could understand Annette's distress. They saved their anxiety for the winter greens that were frost bitten or the firewood that was dampened by the snow.

On the third day Annette and Yann sat at home and waited. They tried to imagine what the disappeared do. Was she lost? Was she rolling in the gutter with a tom cat? Was she dead? Drifting between them were the fears and worries of those who are left behind. Where Blanche had been was now a blank. The cat had been wiped out of their lives as easily as Yann had removed the paint marks from the canvas.

She never returned. Yann didn't finish the painting either. The top right-hand corner was still only a sketch, and the face of the bear who flew over Annette's head possessed a sinister quality which reminded him of Dagarov. He would start again in the city, he said, ripping the canvas off the stretcher. He cut it up into fragments and piece by piece he fed it to the fire.

She packed the bags, she bought the train tickets, she found the apartment and the job. It was a good job, in a couture house on the Avenue Montaigne, a celebrated label uttered in reverence by the magazines that she had read in the small town. Annette stitched light translucent frocks for slim girls who looked like nymphs dancing round the edges of a Greek urn. She beaded the silver screen dresses for film stars to be seen in, and she hemmed the swathes of golden satin for princesses and duchesses to waltz in.

The job was well paid. There was enough money to allow Yann to stay at home in the courtyard apartment and complete his painting, and sufficient for the food which he transformed into dishes they remembered from home. There was even enough for Annette to purchase fabric from the Marché Saint Pierre and make up her own clothes at the weekends. She dressed well in those days in bias cut skirts and blouses with draped collars. She also possessed an evening dress in heavy silk with a narrow banded halter neck, a pleated bodice, and a skirt that brushed the ground. She had nowhere to wear it, for they never went out, but sometimes in the evenings while Yann painted, she would try it on. Wafting around the kitchen or the bedroom she would imagine another life: a life of private railway carriages, yachts, banquets and dances. She would picture half familiar faces that she couldn't name, faces that came from her childhood or from the stories she had read – gentlemen in uniform, ladies in gowns, servants carrying trays of petits-fours and glasses of champagne. But then, knowing that regret eats at you and turns you sour like bad milk, Annette would whisper to herself, 'Things are as they are. They change. They don't change.' And as she trailed the silk frock past Yann once more, she would place a tiny satin kiss on the back of his neck.

He was still labouring at the same painting but he had transformed it by erasing the bear and enlarging the cat in homage to Blanche. The colours had altered too, becoming softer and warmer. As the years passed, he was hopeful that the picture might at last resolve itself, that the problems of proportion could be solved, and the imbalance of colour could be worked out. He hoped that before he grew ill and died he might see the canvas completed.

If only the Germans hadn't come marching into Paris in 1940.

Yann wanted to flee along with all the others. He was itchy with nervousness. He heard echoes in the yard, the click of the catch on a suitcase, the turn of a key in a lock. He wanted to be swept away by the tide of people who rushed southwards along the boulevards to the country roads. He wanted to tie the clothes and the china and the wet canvas to a hand cart and push it all the way back to the slipper factory. He wanted to hide in a barn, in a bed of straw, in a ditch, in a field – anywhere as long as it wasn't the city.

Annette stood with her back to the door and said boldly, 'This time we're not running away.'

She was fearful that if they left they would never return and would be trapped behind vague front lines and borders that ran through muddy farmyards and rivers. She was afraid that the countryside couldn't conceal them. Surely it was better to be hidden in the court-yards and alleys, amongst people, rather than out there alone.

Yann pulled at his brushes and twisted the turpentine cloth in his hand. 'I remember the last time,' he said. 'The massacres and the bodies.'

'So do I,' said Annette. 'But this time I'm not moving.' She pulled a chair away from the kitchen table and sat down on it solidly as if she were guarding the door.

After the soldiers arrived, the city went quiet. The courtyard was silent. No child played. No dog barked. It seemed as if there was no one left but Annette and Yann hidden in the sunless apartment. For days they did not hear the softness of another human voice, only mechanical announcements that were blasted through loudspeakers on the street. When they went outside, they were buried under a flurry of posters and handbills loaded with commands, and they were hounded by the snarls of the soldiers speaking in a language they half knew and hated.

Then slowly things became normal again, or that is what they were told. Annette returned to the couture house where she worked until six, and Yann stayed at home behind the black curtains that she had hung at the windows a year before. There was nothing else to be done, and she realised that the word 'occupation' meant just that, continuing the to-ings and fro-ings. Only now one didn't lift one's head too high, speak too loudly, or catch the eyes of anyone else.

Worries nudged at Annette all the time, like elbows in her ribs. What about food? What if there was nothing to eat? And what about their papers which hadn't been cheap: the price of an emerald ring? She had been told that they were faultless. Their nationality had been transformed and his religion erased. But still she held her breath when the soldiers appeared, stepping straight-legged in front of her. She waited to be stopped; she almost expected it. Her imaginary soldier, something remembered from the past, would be an officer: spotless, smart and heel-clicking. He would have an eyeglass which he would pull out of his pocket and balance on his face, clenching it between his brow and his cheek in a grimace. He would inspect her papers like a cat looking at a mouse, glaring at the words and the handcrafted stamps. Then he would gently take her arm like a solicitous shop assistant or a bank clerk and say, 'This way, Madame, please.'

For Yann, however, the work went well. Perhaps it was because of the quiet of the empty building and the hushed courtyard. The canvas on the wall was almost finished, almost perfect. Another week, he promised himself. All that remained to complete were the two figures in the centre. He had roughly sketched his own portrait, but Annette was still a white shadow amidst the animals.

He mentioned it to her one night. 'It's nearly done,' he said when she came in, pulling off her coat and hat.

She must have been weary or hungry or both for she snapped at him in reply. 'Is that all you can think about?' she cried. 'There are more important things right now, but you can't see them, can you?' The words poured out. 'I remember when you told me that you wanted to be left alone to think what you like. Well no one's going to leave you alone now, and you can't think what you like, not any more. So what are you going to do about it?' She pointed a shaking finger at him.

Yann stood by his canvas feeling the sharpness of her words like a jab from a kitchen knife. He said nothing and the only sound in the apartment came from the clock on the mantelpiece. Counting fourteen ticks, Yann flung down the brush that he held in his hand and walked out of the room.

The anger never lasted long. Later, lying in the dark, Annette regretted her fury. She turned over and looked at him, wishing to say something caring, but he was asleep. His lips were slightly parted and his eyes were shut. Then next day she woke late and there was no time to say anything then either. She left him in a hurry, buttoning her coat in the street and pulling her hat down onto her head.

That day, Yann tidied his brushes and paints away. He knew that she was right. Even as a child he had tried to wriggle his way out of the world and discover places where he couldn't be found. He had edged his way through life, living in the pages of his sketch book and in the marks of the painting. He had avoided, evaded and escaped. Perhaps it was time to learn new words.

He took the shopping basket and, as he walked away from the apartment, he tried out unfamiliar sounds: commitment, confrontation, action. He recited them as he walked further and further out of the city, but the new words didn't seem to fit in his mouth, and he continually tripped and stumbled over them.

By lunch time he had reached the canal. Pausing for a moment, he looked at his foreshortened reflection in the water. There was the same face, he thought, hair still cut in the same way, receding a little at the front perhaps. He looked down at the boy mirrored in the water of the canal. Could he fight? Could he crawl out at night to sabotage a train? Could he camp in the woods and hide in the hills?

Yann climbed up the steps to the metal footbridge that crossed the canal and stood looking over the railings. In the distance, he noticed three men walking towards him, two soldiers and a civilian. The civilian was tall and wore a brown mackintosh. He appeared relaxed beside the Germans, uninhibited and carefree. They stepped onto the bridge, and Yann heard the man laugh. The sound came to him, gently at first, carried by the breeze, but as the man drew closer the laughter became mocking and violent. Yann froze. He knew that laugh. It was a laugh with weight, a laugh with boots on, a mouse-crushing laugh, and instantly the boy was back in the basement with the gold bands around his wrists and his neck. The man came towards him and blinked slowly, then his eyes focused in recognition. He stared at the boy while the soldiers leaned over the railings and watched two women walking along the edge of the canal. The man stared at Yann for a long time, until the youngest soldier tapped his arm. Then he wheeled round and the three men walked away together.

'It was Dagarov,' said Yann that night. 'He knows I'm here in the city. He knows who I am.' Then he added more quietly, 'He knows what I am,' and all the screaming fears returned.

She put her hand on his shoulder. 'You'll never see him again. He doesn't know where we live.'

'He could have followed me,' Yann replied.

She laughed at the boy softly. ' I'm sure he has better things to do.'

The following evening when Annette returned, the apartment was empty and the door was open as if he had just taken the rubbish out or gone to buy some bread. She sat in her hat and coat, resting her head in her hands, her elbows on the table. Looking around the room, she noticed that the shopping basket was stashed by the sink and his jacket was hanging over the back of a chair.

Then she saw the picture. The paint on the canvas was shining moistly. At some time during the day he had painted his own portrait, but his face, unlike the rest of the picture, had been executed in a realistic style verging on the photographic. He must have used the smallest brushes, smoothed the paint across his features, and mixed the subtlest tints to create the roundness, and the dips and hollows. Now the entire canvas was filled apart from her own white face.

The clock on the mantelpiece chimed eight, nine, and ten, and the hands moved slowly round until she was so tired that she couldn't see them at all. She waited at the table all night, dozing sometimes and letting her head drop. In the morning she merely washed her face and brushed her hair before leaving the apartment to catch the bus to work.

On the second evening she waited again, but by then she knew he wasn't coming back. Later she would say that she could feel it. She knew that the cobweb thread had been broken for ever, somewhere between the apartment and where he now lay. She waited another two days before she told the police. What did it matter if they hauled her in too? Nothing mattered any more.

They never found him. He must have been taken north to the suburbs, and then east to the place where the disappeared went. When the war was over and a few of them began to return, she waited at the station, just in case. Then she stood in the foyer of the Hotel Lutetia on the other side of the river, but she never saw him again.

NATHALIE

I can still picture Ania's face with the ditch of a scar across her cheek and the tiny fragment of pastry at the corner of her mouth. She looks at me, waiting, I think. So I tell it straight. I tell it as they told me, in the garden where the dead leaves rolled over the soggy lawns, and in the stale bread, cold tea kitchen on the Hammersmith road.

When I was six years old, my mother went missing. She just disappeared. She vanished on the day that I found the soil-grimed nickel in the rockery. I simply replaced one thing with another, five cents for my mother. At first I wasn't dissatisfied with the exchange, for unlike the empty sucking depression I had felt sitting on that other mother's knee at the children's party two years before, I was not unhappy and I did not weep. The discovery of the nickel filled the void for several days and it was only as the soil gradually disappeared from the creases of my fingers that I began to realise that something wasn't right.

She must have left just as I buried my hand in the mass of leaves and dry shallow roots. She might have seen me, head down, bottom up, as she walked away beyond the boundary of the blue woods to somewhere else. I played amongst the stones until the rain began to darken the granite rocks. Maybe by then my mother had reached town.

Maybe by the time the skin of my hands was scrubbed half-clean, she was sitting on the train, a magazine open on her lap. I can remember that evening when the maid locked my fingers tight in her own, forced them under the water, then scraped the bristles of the nail brush over the soap and applied them to my fingers. She let out sharp irritating sighs that scoured me like the brush while I watched the drops of dirty water mark the white porcelain basin like brown blood.

It was only after several days that I really began to notice my mother's absence. I had probably lost the coin by then, or it had been taken away. I had a nasty habit of putting objects in my mouth 'to test their flavour' as I had once told my father. The nickel had either been placed on the mantelpiece in my bedroom, which at that time I could not reach, or had been removed completely. It was only then that I began to wonder where she was.

Her absence was not an unusual occurrence. She had spent time in hospital, brief spells that no one remarked upon. I wouldn't have known that they occurred at all but for the occasional appearance of a small packed suitcase in the hall that was collected by the gardener and carried out to the car.

Then, there was the delayed honeymoon in Europe. I remember that they sent me postcards of the sights, and on the back, written clearly in my father's hand, were descriptions of where they had been and what they had done.

'Mummy went shopping down this street' or 'Daddy visited this museum.'

From the postcards, I constructed in my mind a continent of endless pavements. There was no countryside in Europe, I concluded. One was condemned to wander for ever along avenues and boulevards, chased by reflections like ghosts in the black of the shop windows. I have always imagined my parents together on these streets, my father straight and upright, my mother stooping a little, wrapped in trembling green silk from head to toe, the ends buffeted by the breeze.

I spent that Christmas with my mean-mouthed, tight-fisted grandmother. She said she was too tired to wait up on Christmas Eve and fill my stocking with gifts, so instead she presented them to me formally at the breakfast table where I was supposed to display restrained curiosity or joy at appropriate points during the meal. She did not believe in enjoyment; life was to be endured. A walk was a means of getting somewhere; food was simply fuel for the body. At mealtimes she pecked at bird portions with her fork and expected me to do the same. The pleasure of eating was something she could never comprehend, and I was scolded for stuffing my mouth full, or peeling the frosting from the cakes, or licking my fingers clean after eating a peach.

I often wonder if my mother had suffered in her relationship with my grandmother, and whether that stiff-backed respectability had affected her too and coloured her own relationship with me. My mother and I spent little time in each other's company. We went shopping sometimes, and on rare occasions she would call for me in the afternoons, but for most of the time she was like a mist in the distance, at the end of the corridor or in another room.

I don't think she liked me much. Even at an early age I sensed it, the way an animal can, through skin or bones. I didn't articulate this belief. I never formed words in my head, but I knew intuitively that she was wary of me. Yet I still loved her. It was the sound of her in the house that I missed when she had gone, the sound of her in other rooms far away from my bedroom.

After she left, my father told me nothing at first, and I didn't ask. I knew better than to pose difficult questions. I played the good little girl for him. When I was invited to his study, or to lunch, or to dine with him, I crossed my legs at my ankles and held my hands in my lap. I kept my mouth shut and I smiled. Sometimes he smiled back absently.

I did ask the maid about her once. It was one of those long dragging mornings in winter. I was sitting on the bed while she buckled my shoes. Through the crack in my bedroom door I could see past the landing into my mother's room and I noticed that the curtains twitched slightly in the cold.

'Where has she gone?' I asked, looking down at the maid's brown-braided head.

Her response was as sharp and as ineffectual as the nail brush with which she had attacked my fingers six months earlier.

'She's ill. Now go and tidy your hair before your father sees you.'

That was the year I played with the music box on my mother's dressing table. I would push my little finger into the edges where the residue of powder still lay and smear it across my face. Then I would try on her shoes, which were disappointingly large. My feet always slipped about inside them. Sometimes, if I felt brave, I would take out the dresses and cloaks that had been draped around coat hangers in the dark closet. When they were pulled over my shoulders they looked like the sagging, shapeless gowns of a medieval lady. I would strut between the dressing table and the bed like the Queen of England, all the time listening for the maid's footsteps along the hallway. I think at those moments I wasn't sorry that my mother was gone.

My father did eventually speak to me about her, but that was a long time later. We had taken the canoe out, and pushed it through the reed beds to the water. Usually he went alone, early in the morning, long before I was up. Only in the summer would he invite me to join him. He would hand me the half-size paddle and carry me into the front of the canoe. But that morning in April, he had asked the maid to wake me, and later, when I was dressed, he and I walked down the hill, our shoes and socks soaked by the dew hanging from the reeds. He helped me into the wobbling canoe and then pushed the stern into the creek and leapt in behind me.

For a while he stayed silent, as if he were waiting until we were a long away from the house before he uttered the lie. It was as if he knew that her silk frocks would rustle in shock and that her gloves in the drawers would twist into knots if they heard the untruths. We rounded the corner of the creek and pulled the canoe onto the bank to look at the flowers. Then he unpacked sandwiches and coffee while

I chattered about the honeysuckle blossom: the flowers were like faces, I said, and the stamens curled out of the petals like tongues.

He watched the clouds pass across the sun, and a ribbon of ducks fly across the creek. Then he turned to me, and asked if I remembered my mother.

Did he really think that children were so dull-witted and forgetful? I didn't know how to reply because the truth was that I thought about her every day: the sound of her voice, her perfume and her clothes. I didn't tell him this. I didn't say anything.

He turned away and looked over the water again. Then he began to speak quickly. He explained that she was sick, and that the sickness had crept inside her and hollowed her out. He said that she slept like Sleeping Beauty, but there was a small chance that the doctors might discover a cure. They were looking for one right now, hunting it out, and if they found it maybe she would wake and get better. He tried to smile reassuringly. I suppose he had to leave a small opening in his story, just in case she came back in her worn down shoes and tattered green suit.

I didn't say anything. Crouching down on the mud, I washed my hands in the river. Then I looked at our house on the hill. It was as small as a doll's house, white and austere. I thought about the scale of things: honeysuckle flowers as big as a face, a house that you could hold between your fingers. I let the thoughts float, like my hands floated in the water, then I pictured my mother. I would have liked to have seen her in the hospital, but I didn't suggest it. I was too polite.

By the time I found the courage to ask, I was told that she was dead.

My father told the second lie eleven years later.

We had just returned from Europe and I suppose he had given up hope that she would ever reappear. Perhaps he realised that even if she did come home, suitcase in hand, he would turn her away. He might have argued that we were better off without her now.

He invited me into his study. It was a velvet room with plush walls and thick carpets, and there was the odour of cigar smoke trapped in the folds of the curtains and in the creases on the button back chairs. He sat at the desk, and in his hands he held a letter that he folded and unfolded as he spoke. I know now that the paper he clutched had nothing to do with our conversation, but at the time it added to the veracity of the scene. One could imagine that it was a letter from a doctor or a faithful nurse or the undertaker.

She had died at last, he said. It was a relief for him. And for her, he added.

'It was no life,' he told me.

I remember that I began to cry. I had saved my tears for eleven years, adding to them month by month, and in the study they exploded in a downpour like the Paris rain. Embarrassed, he called for Sadie and she, innocent and untainted by the lies, led me to the kitchen and wiped my face.

After that, my carapace grew. It was not like his calloused yellow carapace; mine was Cellophane, as fine as the shell of a baby snail. As the years passed it hardened to mother of pearl or coloured glass. I pictured it like the opaline vase on the sideboard in the dining room, cold to the touch and opaque. It remained hard and faultless for a long time, until the crack appeared in Paris, just like the fissure I had imagined in Ania's clam shell.

Sometimes I wonder why he eventually told me the truth. I suppose that, inside his old man's head, there was some need for a deathbed confession or a desire to die guiltless, except that by unburdening himself, he burdened me.

In the nursing home garden he told me that he regretted his lies. He told me that all the time I had thought that she was dead, she was really alive, thinking, or not thinking, about me. While he talked, I looked at the boats on the water – the last things that one sees before the curve of the earth hides the view – and I thought that I should have felt her living. Even if she was out of sight, I should have felt her somewhere in the world. I realised that all the times that she had flitted across my mind like a ghost, she had in fact been leading an ordinary life, maybe reading a book or buying a pair of stockings or washing her face. It seemed remarkable to me that I had felt nothing at all. I should have reached out for the thread that connected us, however fragile it might have been. Or I should have burrowed down into the earth of his lies, through the tangle of leaves and roots, to find the dull depressing nickel of truth. Instead, I had been persuaded into passiveness. I had been a good girl and had never asked questions. My need to conform, to behave well, had overridden any itching curiosity. I was complicit.

He was astonished by my fury. He had done it for the best, he said. As he listed his muddled reasons, the blanket that covered his knees slipped a little and he grabbed at the fringed edges hopelessly. A pale blue nurse stepped past the rose beds with a tray in her hand, while I sat back in the wicker chair to catch my breath.

It was when the rose petals began to brown that he told me this.

The day she left, she carried a suitcase down the drive to the road that was edged by the blue woods. I was playing in the rockery. He was in town. The gardener was in the glasshouse and the maid was in the kitchen reading a cheap magazine. My mother walked down the drive wearing a green dress, a neat cloche hat that covered her hair, and short yellow gloves. In one hand she held a jacket that matched the dress, in the other was a small suitcase packed with underwear and jewels. Over her arm were the straps of a brown leather bag which contained a large sum of money. These were my father's words. He hated to name figures.

'She carried in her brown leather bag a large sum of money.'

The Missing

It had been carefully planned. She had plotted her departure step by step, from the first step she took in the bedroom as she rolled the bracelets inside her silk camisoles to the last step out of the garden gate. No one saw her leave, no one saw her purchase a ticket at the station. She simply dissolved, just melted away into that September afternoon.

She did write him a note that vaguely explained why she was leaving. He discovered it propped against his lamp in the study. He opened it late that night, slitting the envelope across the top with his ivory letter opener. All he found inside was one piece of notepaper on which was written a few un-punctuated phrases that ran into one another. After he read them, he must have crumpled the paper in his hand and let it fall on the floor, or perhaps he tore it into pieces, for strangely, my meticulous father said that he had lost the note.

In the garden of the nursing home, he apologised for being unable to recall properly the contents of the letter. He was certain that she had said very little, just that she wanted a change.

'There was nothing about me?' I asked.

'No, I'm sorry, Frances, nothing.'

She must have written the note directly after lunch. She would have gone to his study and written it there after closing the door quietly behind her. She must have sat in his chair, leaning her hand on his blotter as she wrote. At that time I would have been taking my nap upstairs with the thin curtain pulled across my bedroom window. I hated that early afternoon penumbra. I would lie in bed looking up at the filtered light, listening to the birds outside, or I might walk my fingers dozily across the patterns printed on the bed cover. They were little pink bouquets of flowers, I remember.

After she had finished writing she must have left the study, and crept upstairs softly in order not to wake me. She must have decided to leave while I was sleeping. Did something hold her back? Did she open my door a little as she passed and peer in at my sleepy face, and did she stay too long? Did the telephone ring? Was there a change of plan? Did she sit on the edge of the bed waiting, thinking or regretting? Or was the packing protracted? Could she not decide what to fold into the suitcase? Did she pull out all those dresses and lay them over the bed? Did she open the drawers of her dressing table? Did she lift the lid of the music box for one last time?

Normally the maid would wake me at half past two and then I was permitted to roam around the garden on my own until tea time. My ramblings were limited however. I was not allowed to slip into the fields, or sneak off to the banks of the creek. I was not allowed to enter the glasshouse, or the shed where the rat poison and the weedkiller was kept. I was not allowed, at that age, to play on the swing unattended. I was not allowed to go into the woods, although I would never have gone there, not even close. The shadows were blue-black, and in the afternoon, as the sun moved round, they fell across the bottom of the garden, creeping across the grass. There were large moths that lived there too, camouflaged by the tree bark. Sometimes the shadows were so dark that the moths must have thought it was night, for you could see them seeping, like faint smoke, out of the forest.

The rock garden where I could so easily graze my hands and knees was not out of bounds. I was permitted to clamber over the granite and trample the plants that grew in the dirt. The rockery was my Himalayan mountain range, its crevices filled with saxifrage and phlox. Or it was an island on which I was stranded, or it was a beach with rock pools. From the top of the highest stone, I could see right down to the creek almost to the shingle islands where the colonies of piebald shell ducks and moor hens fed at the edges of the mud. If I turned and looked the other way, there was the wood, and the road that seemed to curve into it.

When she left, she must have seen me, a small blue figure hiking over the stones. She must have heard my voice as I sang to myself. Surely she must have turned her head to the right a little to take a look at the creek that was always as bright as steel in the afternoons. Then she would have seen the blue pinafore dress, my fat white legs, my copper hair. It was the last time that she would see her child. Did she feel nothing at all?

THE WOMAN IN THE
BUTTERFLY DRESS

It all began in another garden, the garden at Ashedene: that was how
Vivien told it. She started right at the beginning amongst the flower
beds and the hedges, in the formal garden that had been laid out
thirty or forty years before. Playing there, running along the paths and
hiding behind the lilacs and the magnolia were two children, Nathalie
and Edward, the elder sister and the younger brother. Nathalie was
my mother's name, a name I have never liked. When I hear its sound,
I picture a piece of dusky pink chiffon caught on a stretch of barbed
wire. I imagine it fluttering like a torn flag on a battlefield.

Nathalie was a pretty girl, light-voiced and lisping. She was her
father's *petite princesse*. There was a photograph of her constrained in
a belted frock and buckled shoes, clutching a tight posy of flowers in
her hands. It was a picture of a soft focused fantasy world, a pale-eyed
perfect child pinned still in front of a painted window and trompe
l'oeil curtain. *Ma petite Princesse, 1905,* he had written on the back of
the curly-edged photograph that he kept inside his pocket book.

If she dusted the books in the library or polished the door knobs,
Nathalie was occasionally her mother's 'good girl', but the words were
almost certainly uttered begrudgingly by my grandmother. The two
did not get on. Mother and daughter sniped and snapped at each
other whenever they met, usually over the lunch and dinner table.
They bickered and exchanged quick sharp retorts, the daughter

hissing insults and names. When the disputes became too knotted and confused they would appeal to my slack-spined grandfather at the top of the table, but he always sided with his princess.

Despite the photographic image of her as the model child, the young girl's moods seemed to swing like the branches of the orchard trees in the wind. She could be as gentle as her sentimental father, she could be domineering and bossy in the company of her brother, or she could be fastidious and prim like her mother. As she grew older, when her face began to take on a shape of its own rather than a disjointed echo of those of her parents, her character too became defined and less changeable. It was as if she had pigeonholed her moods into two distinct slots. Nathalie remained, but when my mother was eleven or twelve years old, another girl began to emerge. For Nathalie was also Natty.

She signed herself Natty on Christmas cards to special friends, or on the covers of her exercise books, and on the first page of her diary. She was Natty when she took a pair of dressmaking scissors and cut off all her hair. She was Natty when she built dens in the hedges, climbed trees or threw snow-covered stones at her brother. She was Natty when she wrote the plays they performed outside in the garden where their speeches were blown away by the breeze, or inside on the galleried landing that led to the bedrooms. She never performed herself. She was above mere imitation. Natty was the inventor of another world. She always stood back behind a box hedge or in one of the bedrooms, whispering directions and forgotten lines to the players.

In those days there were two other children who visited the garden in the summer, but they were quieter and less boisterous. They didn't feel quite at home in the alleys of pleached lime trees and they were uncomfortable under the sharp-eyed gaze of my grandmother. Cousin Vivien and her brother Frank were city children who came for the holidays. Ostensibly sent away from the heat and the smell, they were consigned to Ashedene for two months so that their parents could travel abroad. Vivien and Nathalie were almost the same age: they hated each other and they adored each other. In the first days of the summer they spat and sulked, but at the end of the holiday Nathalie wept when the train pulled Vivien out of the station and back to the city.

Frank was older, an adolescent with a broken voice. Awkward with both adults and children, he would walk stiffly away from Natty's games, constantly aware of his hands which seemed to have a life of their own. They would flap by his side, or reach up and rub his pimpled chin, his mouth or the end of his nose. He would try and contain them in his pockets, but often he would push them down so far into the cloth that they would tear the seams.

The Ashedene garden where Natty and Vivien played was the remnant of a much greater estate that had been parcelled up and sold off slowly during the children's lives. After the century turned, things did not go well for my grandfather.

Henri Leonard had been born in a town in northern France, near the Belgian border, but, because his family had emigrated in the first year of his life, he had no real memories of the country at all. This was perhaps why he venerated everything French – lacy poetry and music, pastel paintings and rich cloying food. It was just as well, however, that he never visited his birthplace because he would have been disappointed. There was nothing of the Symbolists or the Impressionists there, just a grey sky – thick as a blanket – and a ring of factories around a town square where the cafés served tripe-sausage and beer.

The Leonard textile factory founded by his father in the town of Longpoint produced bed and table linen: machine embroidered sheets and tablecloths that were embossed with flowers, monograms and scalloped edges. The business had done well at first, and Ashedene was built on land that adjoined the factory. The construction of the house was followed by the digging of the gardens and the purchasing of fields and farms nearby. When all was complete, the prospect from the windows of the dining room at Ashedene was as fine as from any eighteenth century English country home. The formal gardens drifted away into the meadows, and there were no ugly high hedges or fences that obstructed the view. Everything, it seemed, as one stood looking out of those brocade-curtained windows, was within the grasp of the Leonard family.

When Henri took over, however, things began to turn bad. He had never been interested in sums. To him numbers had no meaning; they were only shapes on the page that remained immutable and refused to be multiplied and divided. As a consequence of this, he relied too heavily on his managers, who managed badly, and then there were problems with the unions and the war. After the death of his son, Edward, Henri Leonard retreated into his collection of paintings and prints and the French poetry books that were kept in the library. Refusing to converse in English any more he lost himself in the light-tipped delicate tongue rolls of French. He found refuge in the language that no one but his daughter spoke.

I think it was then that my grandmother perfected her puritanism, cutting down on food, walking rather than taking the car, biding her time, knowing that the fall was inevitable. In the last month of my grandfather's life, the factory was bought for almost nothing by a consortium from the city. Next, Ashedene was sold and swiftly demolished, and the land divided into small lots. The day that Nathalie became engaged to my father, the box hedges were ripped out and the rose beds flattened. The day she married him, nothing remained of the garden at all and the view had disappeared for ever.

It was fortuitous that my mother was rescued from the wreckage. If she had remained unmarried, she would surely have suffered in the small apartment taken by my grandmother. It was a miserable place that housed the few relics gathered from Ashedene: the ghastly elongated art-nouveau vases and the statuettes that caught the dust and threw grotesque shadows on the walls. In one of the rooms were a number of tea chests containing books from my grandfather's library that nobody had bothered to unpack. The chests were piled on top of one another in unsteady columns, and if one opened the door and entered the room they shuddered unhappily against the walls.

My father carried Natty/Nathalie off to Bluewood in the spring of 1917. They were married in the church on the other side of the creek. It was a warm day and after the ceremony Natty decided that they should walk back to the white house rather than taking the car. I can imagine them now, wandering up the lane to the house followed by their guests: my father in his morning suit and my mother dressed in her wedding gown, with a bunch of orange blossom in her hands. I can see her hair, red against the white silk of her dress, and her pale face framed by the blue woods in the distance.

I think my father loved Natty the most: madcap Natty, sparkling Natty. She was the pretty girl, the giggler and the practical joker. Natty could turn somersaults and could sprint faster than the men. When it was warm she would dive from the jetty and swim from one side of the creek to the other, and sometimes she would take the canoe out and paddle furiously down the river, her hair streaming behind her.

Only occasionally was she over-shadowed by her other persona.

By then Nathalie had grown increasingly morose. She had become a disturbing adult version of the party-frocked girl in the photograph, stiff and silent, her hands locked together in her lap. On bad days, Nathalie would sit in the drawing room without moving or speaking, and sometimes my father would bring her books or magazines to read. He would slip the book between her hands and turn the pages for her. But after a while, he realised that there was nothing he could do or say that would change her mood.

I think that in the early days of their marriage he was happy. When I was clearing the study, I found letters and notes in his desk drawer that must have been written just after their marriage. My father called my mother 'his precious' and 'his jewel'. 'To my golden girl,' he wrote, or 'Dearest diamond.' These endearments were always followed by promises: he told her he would buy her a closet full of dresses, and that they would travel to Europe when the war was over, they would shop in Paris and visit galleries in London.

The honeymoon was postponed, however, for I was conceived with embarrassing speed soon after the wedding. In the first few weeks of the pregnancy my mother felt quite ill and she lost interest in redecorating the house, or planning the planting of the garden. To make things worse, she discovered that she could no longer fit into the slim gilded dresses my father had bought her. She had developed an unfashionable cleavage and a large bulge around her middle and was forced to wear loose gowns and soft slippers. And finally, after nine months of bloated misery, vomiting, backache and swollen feet, she was presented with a cringing pink-skinned, blue-veined baby.

From the instant she had imagined me in her womb, I had become an impediment to her own pleasure. As soon as I was born in the blood and the viscera of that dreadful summer night, I terrified her and she despised me. My mother refused to look at me. I was wrinkled, creased and unrecognisable as her own. She saw something other than a howling baby. She saw horns on my head, drooling fangs in my mouth, or she saw a limbless crawling maggot.

My father found solutions. Nathalie was taken to hospital and soothed with medication. He hired a nurse for me, a crisp cotton woman with a commanding voice. For months, Nathalie/Natty came and went. Nathalie sat in bed, staring blankly at the nurse who powdered the baby's bottom and changed her nappy, and Natty, more impulsive and excited than ever, also made an appearance. She would scoop the baby from the nurse's arms and throw her in the air with cries of hysterical affection.

'Sweet baby. Lovely baby.'

After a year or so, my mother's health began to improve. She was stable enough to care for me, although the nurse remained in the house until my father decided that I was safe – too big to be easily drowned in the bath and too strong to be smothered with a pillow. Then as I grew older my mother and I eyed each other cautiously. She tried hugging me, but the loops of beads she wore around her neck pressed against my stomach and made me squirm. She read me stories and sang me songs, but after a while she grew bored. In the end, she did what she could, what she knew best. She took me shopping. Nathalie liked to buy me presents. She would wrap them so carefully with the paper folded and pleated and the ribbons knotted into rosettes. Yet she was rarely there to smile at my excitement when I unwrapped them. She was always somewhere else down a corridor or in the garden talking with someone else.

When I was four and a half, my father took her to Europe as he had always promised, and she adored it. She told him that she had never felt so at home as she did under the colonnades of the Louvre, or in the small tea room on the rue de Rivoli. She was appreciated by the waiters and the shop girls for her pretty face and the fluency of her French. She said that people seemed to like her there and she felt understood. My mother spent hours just strolling, looking in the windows of shops and picking out gifts for herself and for her family. That was when she must have visited the embroidery *atelier* and purchased the shawl.

It was Vivien who told me that my mother had remained in the shop for some time, examining the items on display, fascinated by the stitches and the colours. They were so unlike the clumsy, mechanical white work on the Leonard tablecloths and sheets. Natty bought the shawl for Vivien, and my father bought my mother an embroidered bed jacket, a short, sashed kimono in china blue silk. A garden had been embroidered over the cloth, a pattern of plants that grew from the hem of the jacket before spiralling around the arms and the body, and snared in the tiny silk spaces between the stems and the blossom were insects, birds and butterflies.

At first she was delighted with the jacket. She loved it so much that in London, she wore it to a dinner party over an evening gown, much to my father's embarrassment. But following the return to dreary Bluewood the jacket came to represent something more sinister, as if it had been endowed with bad magic. Having unpacked and distributed her gifts to me, the maid and the gardener, she retreated to her bed and took breakfast, lunch and dinner on a tray like an invalid. Now she was Nathalie, and Nathalie refused to rouse herself, saying that she wouldn't get up until the summer, until she felt the warmth of the sun on the bedclothes.

In the dark afternoons, if she wasn't drowsing, her head lolling against the pillow, she would follow the raised silk pattern on her bed jacket. Compulsively her finger would trace the swirls and pirouetting stems. If I sat on my own bed with the door open, I could see her arm moving round and round and I could hear the faint brush of silk against silk. It seemed that she was compelled to follow the stitches. It was as if she were bewitched, for as I crept closer to the door to watch her face, I could see she was immersed by the endless task, her finger lost in the labyrinth of patterns.

My worried father misinterpreted her actions and bought her a length of silk, some thread and an embroidery hoop. He hoped that she would make designs inspired by the garden on her jacket and that the act of creating something of her own might drag her out of the maze. But she ignored the package that was placed gently on the bed beside her, and she didn't listen to what he said. Later he unwrapped the fabric, the needles and the frame. He draped the silk over his arm to show off its sheen, then fitted a section of it into the grasp of the hoop. She didn't touch the cloth, however, and after he left, it slid to the floor and was kicked inadvertently under the bed by the maid when she brought in the supper tray.

My mother lay in bed for months, her fingers following the embroidered lines on the blue silk, just as her feet had followed the narrow garden paths at Ashedene. As time passed the plants and flowers on the jacket seemed to grow like a jungle and the wiry stems knotted around her torso and her arms. Rather than silk, she now felt damp leaves against her skin, and she smelt the heavy scent of the jungle flowers. Nathalie was constrained by the stitched garden and covered by the long-stemmed flowers that would gradually pull her to the ground.

She wrote to Vivien saying that she could feel the ivy tightening itself around her waist, around her wrists like handcuffs, and throttling her neck. She said that she was tied to the bed, and the only things she could move now were her fingers. She said that my father had bound her there while he seduced the maid and the gardener's wife.

'He makes love to them all, while I lie here pinned down by the stems. And the flowers and leaves won't stop talking. And the silk bugs fly round my head. He's tied me up so I cannot move.'

Vivien was appalled by the letter. She cabled my father and in short cursory phrases explained its contents.

Yet Nathalie was not taken to hospital. Against all advice, my father chose to have her treated at home, and each morning a doctor arrived but without the usual doctor's bag. He twittered and scurried, as grey as the mice I had seen in the garden shed. From my bedroom I would watch him scuttle along the landing and enter her bedroom and shut the door behind him with a click. No one explained to me how he finally loosened the ivy strands that fastened her to the bed. At some point, I suppose, my mother must have removed the bed jacket, or maybe the doctor took it away and replaced it with something innocuous made of wool or lace. Maybe then she got up and started to move around the bedroom again. Maybe she sat at the dressing table and applied lipstick and rouge, then dusted the powder from the music box over her neck and face. Some time later she must have fluttered onto the landing and down the stairs to lead a half-normal life again. But in the end she fooled them all, for on that clear day in

September, she left the note on the desk and walked off, down the road, with a suitcase in her hand.

I asked Vivien whether Nathalie had had a lover, but she replied that it wasn't possible. For months my mother hadn't shifted from her bed and had communicated only with my father and the doctor.

'What about their holiday in Paris?' I asked, imagining a stream of dapper-moustached young men following giggling Natty down the rue de Rivoli.

'That wasn't possible either,' said Vivien. 'Your father never left her alone.' Apparently he had worried that my mother might dart off into a side street. Or that she might lose herself in the long narrow arcades, or along the tree lined paths of Père-Lachaise.

So the contents of the small suitcase – the jewels and the under- wear – did not indicate an amorous liaison, or a lascivious romance where outer clothes were not required. The image that I had held in my head of my mother in a silk camisole and diamonds at her throat, floating on a blue bed as big as the sea, was thankfully false. Her negli- gent packing was simply a sign of an irrational mind.

They looked for my mother in the woods. They checked the banks of the creek for a washed-up, green-wrapped body. They scanned the edges of the railway tracks and the road sides. They read through the lists of patients in hospitals and sanatoria. But she wasn't there.

My father hired his own detective, a man called Diver. I can picture him now: a tall blue suit, hat in hand, standing in the doorway to the study.

He said, 'Hello kid,' as I crept through the hall and up the stairs carrying my doll. I didn't answer him. I didn't know who he was.

Diver visited the shops that Natty had loved to frequent: the perfume shops and hat shops and the large emporia in which one could wander for days. He searched through lists of passengers who had crossed the Atlantic, disembarking at Liverpool or Southampton. He checked hotel reservations. But she wasn't there.

Later my father told me that Diver wasn't any good. His expenses had been large, and his reports empty. He drank, he was indiscreet and he bothered the family. Diver had visited my grandmother's apartment, breathing illegal whisky fumes and cigarette smoke into the heavy afternoon air. He must have sat on one of the upright chairs in the drawing room. She would have stood, poker-backed by the fireplace, with her tight little bird's eyes staring down at him. I can imagine Diver, too hot in his blue pinstripe, running his fat finger inside the damp stiff collar of his shirt. I can imagine him asking questions composed of slurred words that slipped out too easily and too loosely. And, as the shadows of the vases and the statuettes shifted with the changing light across the walls, she would have said it was a family matter and would have refused to answer.

The assignment must have been impossible. Diver was hunting for a woman who had simply vanished. My mother had evaporated into the woods, sunk in the creek or was lost in the stitches of an embroidered garden.

There was no trace of her until the day I turned fifteen.

We had taken the canoe to the shingle islands that lay in the middle of the river. It was an established tradition that on our birthdays we would paddle the canoe along the creek and land at the edge of Bagnold's Reach. There we would unload the sandwiches, soda and slices of cake, and we would picnic, leaning against the upturned canoe.

My fifteenth birthday was the day that Frank, my mother's cousin, sent the cable. When we returned from the creek, Sadie met us at the back door. She whispered to my father that a message had arrived and was lying on his desk. And without washing his hands or changing his shoes, he squelched along the hallway to his study, shingle and mud skating across the polished boards.

Twenty five years later in the nursing home, my father told me that Frank had seen Nathalie in France. Or at least he thought he had.

After spending a month with Vivien in London, Frank had decided to visit Paris before returning home. He had never been to the city before and had planned an arduous itinerary for himself. He traipsed from the Louvre to Notre Dame, and from Sacré-Coeur right down to the Pantheon. He strolled through the Tuileries and under the arcades on the rue de Rivoli. He drifted along the river and around the edge of the Ile St Louis and the Ile de la Cité. Then, on the last day of his tour, he walked eastwards across the city to Père-Lachaise.

It was there, in the cemetery, that he saw her.

Frank had been peering at the inscription on a tombstone when he noticed a woman in the distance. She was escorted by a young man who was murmuring gently to her in French. The woman bobbed like a small bird up the grand avenue that led to the crematorium on the hill. In one hand she carried a bunch of pink and white roses, in the other a small blue clutch bag. Her dress was yellow and the collar and sleeves were trimmed with black braid. She was the colour of a butterfly, a Swallowtail, thought Frank.

He stared at the woman, although at first he wasn't sure why she had attracted his attention. As she walked away, up the hill, he decided that there was something about the colour of her hair, the slope of the shoulders and her white freckled hands. There was something about the way she moved. Then a word formed in Frank's mouth, and without thinking he shouted it aloud, 'Natty.'

The couple climbed up the steps towards the crematorium, then turned off onto a path that meandered amongst the gravestones and the tombs. As he followed them, Frank was certain that they had turned right by the statue of the veiled weeping woman. He had seen the hem of the yellow frock flickering through the gaps between the stones. He was positive he had heard Natty's voice drifting down to him through the leaves, but when he reached the summit he found he was alone. He looked around, confused, but there was no one there, only a cat who pushed through the buddleia and slunk past him down the steps. The man and the woman had disappeared.

My father chose an agency with associates in Paris. They employed detectives who specialised in these sorts of cases: missing people and runaway husbands and wives. They warned him that there was very little to go on.

'Please don't get your hopes up, sir,' they said.

He heard nothing for a month, so he began impatiently to devise his own plans that gradually involved me. He told me that he had bought tickets for Europe, and pushing the end of his pen along the map draped over his desk, he outlined a journey through Italy and France to England. I think he had expected me to be excited, but I was not. I remembered the postcards, and the everlasting pavements of Europe. I had no desire to walk down those streets, or to browse in shops and dull museums. I was not a sophisticated adolescent. I was happy with the creek, and still frightened of the woods, but it seemed that I had no choice. He sat at his desk with the map in front of him, saying that it would be good for me to travel, it would be something I would never forget. I know now that he was worried that I would grow like her. He wanted to keep me close. He thought I resembled my mother too much.

Perhaps there were other reasons for taking me to Paris. Although he never admitted it, I'm certain that he considered me a useful accessory, a means of wheedling her out of her shell, an encouragement of some sort. I would have been presented to her as a grown up, independent daughter, no longer a creeping maggot. Although I cannot imagine how he would have explained her presence in the city to me, or how he could possibly have resolved his Sleeping Beauty story.

After we crossed the border into France, I noticed that he was distant and agitated. He took photographs without planning the shots, relentlessly clicking the button until the film was all used up. Then he postponed the tour of the chateau we had organised. He said that he was sick, it must have been something he had eaten. He would feel better in Paris, he was sure.

I didn't know that two days earlier in Nice he had received a message. They said that they had found her but had not approached her. They said that in this case it was preferable that her husband was present at the interview. She lived with a Frenchman, they said, in an unfashionable part of the city, on the rue Villiers-L'Isle-Adam, in a large house. Her companion left for work at eight and returned at half past six. She did not leave the house, except to buy flowers from the florists on the rue de Pyrénées or to promenade through the cemetery. My father had known this when the train pulled into the gare de Lyon, and he must have been thinking about it as we tumbled round the city in a taxi. When he left me with the French family at the brick villa in the suburbs he had already organised his rendezvous for the following day.

The woman on the rue Villiers-L'Isle-Adam was not my mother. She stood in her blue salon, surrounded by the hard paste glint of Limoges and Sèvres, and shouted shrilly at my father and the detective. She was angry at the neighbours who had betrayed her, and she was protective of her lover, and her child who sat upstairs in the nursery listening to the row below. The interview was short and embarrassing. When it was over, my father and the detective crept uncomfortably down the hallway and out of the house.

After that he worked alone. For two weeks, he searched the hospitals and asylums. Then he rifled through documents at the Préfecture de Police and in the Town Halls, but he found nothing.

When he finally came to collect me, I was sitting on a garden chair watching the river float away towards the sea. The family in the brick villa had abandoned me to the rotting leaves and the mossy grass. I was pleased to see him and it showed, I think, for his face lit up in the winter sun and he put his arm around me.

'I've come back. It's just you and me now,' he said.

I thought I knew what he meant.

He never tried to find my mother again. The incident on the rue Villiers-L'Isle-Adam had been so humiliating that he never hired another detective. Instead he invented a story for us both. She died, quietly, in a hospital bed. Then she was cremated and scattered on the sea. That was what he told me.

He and I were never so close again. On my sixteenth birthday I didn't join him in the canoe because I had other things planned. I began my own life, which for a while was an uninteresting episode of young men, parties and vague hopes for the future. My father hid from me more and more. He grew shy of me, removing himself to the study, or the canoe. When he couldn't hide, or if I came too close, he would simply put the camera's view finder to his eye and snap away.

When my father told me Nathalie's story in the garden of the nursing home, I became so angry that I had to stop my flailing hands breaking a tea cup or hitting out at him. But after he died, when I cleared the house, I experienced other feelings which grew slowly. I decided that I wanted to be the one that found her. I wanted to find her and shake sense into her. I would do what my father would never do and put a notice in the paper. I had no time for surreptitious list checking or creeping behind the tombs of the cemetery, or wandering aimlessly through the streets searching for a woman who looked like my mother.

When I arrived in the city, I had not expected to feel the sinking dozy-headed lethargy that I experienced in the cafés, the shops and the hotel. I felt as if my legs were made of lead, a sensation I had only ever had in my nightmares when I tried to run from the blue woods. Sitting at the desk or lying on my bed in the hotel room, I was unable to organise my thoughts, find a pen, or open my notebook, and as I walked through the city, I was distracted. I drifted without purpose while I wondered whether I really wanted to find her at all.

THE MISSING

The rain fell again, fine like powder. It was an almost imperceptible ghost rain: muslin thin. There were no pools of water or streams in the gutter, just a gentle dampening of the streets that added a slight sheen to the pavement and mist to the windows. It looked like the end of the rain.

Inside, the room had darkened with the clouds, but I could still see Ania who was sitting, staring ahead blankly, the fingers of her hands clasped together in her lap. She was elsewhere, however, not in the room with me. She hadn't even noticed the change in the weather, the gloom, or the rain outside. For a moment I wondered whether she had listened to anything I had said, and I waited, unsure of how to break the silence. At last she opened her mouth and said softly, 'There was a child. I had a child, not with Yakov, with my husband,' she paused. 'He said I was mad. They said I couldn't look after her. They locked the door. They cut off my hair, made me look like a boy.' Then she shook her head. 'No, that's not right, that was before with the doctor.'

Reaching down to touch the plate, she dipped her finger in the sugar dust and made a spiralling pattern in it. 'My child. My little girl.'

Ania lifted her eyes, then she smiled, but it was only a stretch of the lips, a brief tensing of her facial muscles. It meant nothing.

'All that was a long time ago.' She tried to giggle and a hiccup of sound rose from her mouth and died instantly. 'A long time ago. Things change.'

Levering herself awkwardly from the chair she took the plate into the back room to wash it. I knew from my previous visits that this was the sign that I should leave: she always ran the water over the dish and shouted from behind the flowered curtain, 'You will come again tomorrow, Frances, with a cake?'

But this time, she was silent, and this time I was reluctant to move. I sat looking at the windows. It seemed then that the shop was drifting, and had become detached from the rest of the city by the magic rain and the condensation. I held my breath and waited for her to continue. I knew that if I spoke my voice would kill the mood. I was certain that behind the curtain Ania was at the edge of a precipice looking down at herself. Did she know who she was, or had she forgotten? Had she simply separated one life from another and rubbed out the first? I waited, listening to the running tap and the muffled squeaks of a tea towel against the porcelain. Then I heard the clatter as the plate was stacked on a shelf. I waited a long time, but when Ania returned, her face had changed. It was a mask that was hard and taut, and I knew that if I touched her cheek, the skin would feel cold. She smiled at me brightly as she dried her hands on the tea towel. 'You will come again tomorrow, Frances, with a cake?' she asked.

Later that evening, in my hotel room, I wrote questions on the lined pages of my notebook. Then I whispered them aloud to test the phrasing and intonation, and to guess at the responses. For the first time I felt excitement rising in my throat. I knew that I was close to something that I could almost touch. It was like fumbling for a light switch in a strange room. After weeks of running my hands along black walls, my fingers now touched the edge of the smooth brass casing and all I had to do was to flick the switch.

I put down my pen and raised my head from the notebook. The table at which I sat had been pushed against the window and I hadn't yet drawn the curtains. I looked out. The street below me was empty. There were no cars or cabs, only pedestrians: two women, one holding a shopping bag, the other a rolled umbrella. They walked slowly on either side of the road, now illuminated by the lamplight, now dissolving into the dark. I stood up and leaned against the window frame with my hand on the curtain. The women walked in step, parallel. They moved steadily together in the same direction, but always separated by the darkness of the road. I watched them until my eyes grew tired, and then they seemed to merge and disappear out of sight.

The following morning my optimism faded. I had hoped for sun, but the grey clouds hung low over the city making the buildings flat and the streets shadowless. I cannot be sure, but maybe I already suspected that she would be gone when I bought the cake from the patisserie. And maybe I already imagined that the padlocked shutters would be pulled down to the pavement as I climbed the hill to her street. I called for her, but there was no reply. I stood outside the shop and shouted, conscious of the faces that peered at me from the windows above. I had no wish to ask them about Ania so I walked away, leaving the boxed cake on a doorstep in the hope that someone might pick it up before it spoiled.

When I returned to the hotel, I tried to ignore my confusion and keep my head clear. I sat at the table again and began to type up my notes. They had been hurriedly written the day before, and were riddled with spelling mistakes, abbreviations and blots from my pen. I tapped at the keys and I reasoned with myself: her absence is only an interruption, a hiatus. After all she was unpredictable, she could return tomorrow, next week, any time.

I should have known, however, that the moment I began to believe in Ania she would slip away or evaporate, just like Frank's butterfly woman in the cemetery, or Dagarov's fleeting vision of the face in the bus. The moment we see the light we are instantly plunged back into the darkness again.

I visited the street day after day but she wasn't there. I eventually talked to her neighbours, which wasn't easy because they screwed up their faces as they struggled to distinguish familiar words in my heavily accented French. They couldn't tell me anything. Some said that they had seen her, but had never spoken to her; others hadn't even noticed the dressmaker's shop below their apartments. They were polite, but they shrugged their shoulders and shook their heads.

My frustration dissolved into lethargy. I was aware of strange things that spring: spaces grew smaller, distances longer. My bedroom shrank to the size and proportions of an upturned shoebox, and the roads between the hotel and Ania's shop stretched for ever no matter how fast I walked. Knowing that I had become too solitary and needed company, I decided that I would leave the city for a while.

I wrote to Vivien and suggested a week away. I thought – wrongly as it turned out – that her chatter might do me good. After a short correspondence we settled on a week's holiday on the Normandy coast. It seemed a convenient destination for us both. A few days later I purchased my ticket and then caught the train that ran westwards along the railway beside the brick villa where I had stayed as a child. I searched for the house, but I could not see it. Perhaps it was hidden amongst the new apartment blocks and the factories that edged the river, or perhaps it had been demolished.

The train seemed to stop at every town along the coast. Brief lurches of movement were followed by interminable delays outside wisteria-covered stations, and it took almost three hours to reach Houlgate. I did not know the place and had chosen it simply because its name intrigued me. I had imagined that the town would be bleak and sea swept. I thought that the wind would howl along the beach. But in that April week there was something sulky about the weather and the sea was shy too. It hovered in the distance like a timid child.

We stayed in a turreted hotel which depressed me more than my own hotel in Paris. The rooms possessed an institutional coldness that immediately reminded me of my father's nursing home. And the tiled hallways and galleries emitted a sadness that one normally feels only at the end of the season when the hopes of summer are unfulfilled and one is obliged to return home in disappointment. Vivien seemed to enjoy herself, however, which only made my misery worse. She wandered through the corridors imagining another age: ladies bustled and corseted in dresses of bright silk. She saw them, she said, gliding down the stairs and through the entrance to the promenade with their capes and parasols. She said she could see the fronds of the ostrich feathers in their hats waving softly in the air.

We too walked along the promenade and onto the beach where the sea had banked up piles of sea shells. In the afternoons, with nothing better to do, I picked them up and found Scotch bonnets, baby's ears, moon snails and kitten's paws. I inspected each shell, raised it up to my eyes, and watched the lines of colour spiral into a vanishing point. By the end of the week I had collected an astonishing assortment of colours and intricate shapes: purples and rose pinks, ridged corals, twisting pinnacles, craggy cones. I kept them in the pockets of my raincoat and took them out from time to time. Placing them on the tablecloth in the restaurant or the bedclothes in my room, I arranged them in lines according to type or size.

When I wasn't on the beach, I stared out at the spread of sand and the sea. Slowly, I began to feel better. Now that I was outside the labyrinth of the city and the maze of stories, I was certain again that I could find her. The task seemed so much easier away from the knot of roads and the rain that obscured everything. I started to make lists in my notebook and resolved that my investigations should follow broad straight avenues and boulevards rather than the narrow paths and courtyards that had trapped me.

It was then that I decided that I would rent an apartment when I returned to the city. I would take a small place, I thought, where I could cook for myself if I chose, and write without being disturbed.

The Missing

On my return to Paris, I discovered that all the high-ceilinged apartments on the roads I had admired were either unavailable or too expensive. After a month of hunting, I was finally forced to accept a dingy space on the avenue Ledru-Rollin over a florist's shop. The apartment is on the *entre sol*, sandwiched unhappily between the ground floor and the *belle étage*. As a consequence of this, the deep balconies above me extend so far out over my windows that the sitting room is bathed in shadow for most of the day. Added to this, the bedroom is situated over the main entrance to the block so not only can one hear the noise from the road below but also the comings and going of the tenants as they rattle their bicycles through the entrance to the courtyard at the back of the building.

I ignored all this when I inspected the apartment. There was so little choice that I felt I could not refuse it, and despite the small windows and the dimness, I have remained here ever since, like a mouse hiding in the gap between the ceiling and the floor boards. I cannot imagine dragging myself out of my hole and moving somewhere better. Sometimes I think the furniture has expanded and that no removals company could ever squeeze it out of my tiny windows or my narrow front door. I am stuck here.

I took the apartment in the heavy heat of early June. Then, regularly throughout the summer, I lumbered up the roads to Ania's shop again. It remained empty until the beginning of September, but the new tenant – an upholsterer – could tell me nothing. He stripped away an old yellow brocade that had covered an armchair and shook his head. That was the day I put the notices in the newspaper: two notices under *Avis de Recherches*. One was for Ania Dupuy as she called herself, the other for Nathalie Daye née Leonard. I paid for the announcements to run until Christmas, but received no response to either.

I think, in truth, I did not really expect to find my mother, not that way at any rate. I could not seriously imagine her opening the newspaper and replying to my three-lined request for information. Indeed, I could not be sure that she was in the city at all, or that she had survived the war. And even if she were still alive, I wasn't certain that I wanted to meet her, or hear the explanations for her disappearance. What could she say to the daughter she had left behind? What possible excuse could she give?

There were days when I imagined a conversation of sorts. As I listened to her faint, flat words of explanation, however, I quickly realised that it was not her voice that I heard in my head, but the droning voices of the Anastasias repeating their own misfortunes. During the autumn and winter months of that year, I noticed that the water-colour painting of my mother which I had hung on the wall over the mantelpiece was slowly transforming itself too. Her features shifted and changed with the light and often in the evenings I found myself staring at a portrait of Ania instead.

I waited for a message, for some sort of sign from Ania, but nothing came and I felt hurt and a little betrayed. I began to believe that I had imagined her; after all she was only words on the pages that lay on the desk in front of me. I wondered whether it was possible that she had never existed.

In the spring of the following year, I decided to visit Dagarov once more. He had not replied to the various letters and cards I had sent him concerning Ania, and I was irritated by his silence. Anticipating the same difficulties that I had faced a year before, I arrived early, hoping to catch the concierge before she fell asleep. When I reached Dagarov's building, I discovered to my surprise that the door from the street to the courtyard was wide open, and inside, stacked on the cobblestones, were piles of bed linen, a kitchen table, and a wall cupboard. Beyond all this, sitting in an armchair outside the concierge's apartment, was Irina, dabbing her wet eyes with a dirty tea towel.

The concierge translated for me. She explained that Boris Dagarov had collapsed and died on the platform of the gare de l'Est two weeks earlier. She told me that Boris and Irina had planned to visit relatives, and that Irina had baked a number of large and heavy Easter cakes destined as gifts for her cousins. The cakes had been wrapped in brown paper and packed carefully inside an old cardboard suitcase. It was this suitcase that Dagarov had been lifting onto the train when he collapsed.

'It was like he saw a ghost,' the concierge whispered, looking over her shoulder at Irina. 'His eyes popped and his skin was all white.'

Dagarov had dropped the case, pressed his hand against his heart and had fallen awkwardly into the gap between the platform and the train. The suitcase had burst open and the cakes had rolled solidly away between the legs of the departing passengers.

'Like he saw a ghost,' I thought as I wandered back to my apartment: was it the ghost of a returning deportee trudging back up the platform to find Ania?

Following my visit to Boris Dagarov's building, I realised that I had reached another impasse. After all, Ania had disappeared, Dagarov was dead, and Mikhail Pivkin, who was on the other side of the Atlantic, had not answered my letters. Resolving to forget them and escape the fiction, I organised my notes and filed them inside the cabinet. I wanted to bury them at the back of the drawers. I wanted to stifle Ania's voice that rose from the pages of my notes and hide my mother's face that peered at me from the painting. I had to force them to disappear again; I pushed them down into the dark amongst the bank statements and the gas bills. I wanted to move on and forget. I was tired of writing and rewriting, repeating the same stories. I needed to reinvent myself, to change the way I looked and the way I wrote. I wanted to become someone else, and for a while I succeeded.

THE NOTEBOOK

In the nineteen sixties my restaurant reviews and cookery articles were surprisingly popular. I tried to write the truth, avoiding embroidery and embellishments. I expounded upon the benefits of olive oil and garlic, described the sharpness of *aioli* and *pistou*. I travelled to the south, eating my way through dish after dish of *bouillabaisse*, grilled sardines and breaded egg plant. Then I wrote about the flavours, composing the articles as I sunned myself on a terrace or a balcony that overlooked the sea. I still have the slick coloured photographs that accompanied my articles: mounds of sea food, glasses of rose-pink shrimp, an ochre-coloured soup in a thick-edged terrine. There are pictures of me too, in front of market stalls choosing a lobster or an artichoke. I dyed my hair a shade lighter and wore sunglasses and lipstick. I look shiny and successful, a real magazine woman.

On those trips, I was occasionally accompanied by a companion who had travelled with me from Paris, or someone whom I had met in the hotel or in a restaurant. But those relationships never lasted. They were as fleeting and as transient as my made-up face. I always returned home alone.

Lloyd Harbin used to visit me then, filling those lonely gaps. For brief periods of time I enjoyed his company. He was gentle and mildly amusing. I found that there was something comfortable about the curves of his body and I was no longer repulsed by the permanent dampness above his lips or on his brow. He would visit for two weeks each spring – preferring to stay in a hotel rather than with me in my apartment – and we would spend most days together, rediscovering the city. He liked to walk short distances through the streets, interrupting these journeys with cups of coffee or hot chocolate, and a slice of tarte tatin or a crème brulée. I remember one afternoon in particular: we had lunched together and afterwards had wandered slowly past the bibliothèque towards the Palais-Royale. It was sunny and we decided to sit in the square and watch the light play on the jets of water that sprayed out from the fountain. It was then that he began to talk about the Anastasias.

'Sent you on a wild goose chase,' he said. 'But without them you wouldn't be living in Paris,' and he turned and looked at me saying that it was quite by chance that he had mentioned the Duchess that night at Jack's party.

He had watched me, he said, standing by the fireplace while Jack laughed with another woman, and he had noticed that my eyes were moist. He had seen the tears catch the light. He said that he had taken my arm and pulled me away from the group, desperately trying to think of something to say. He had never imagined that I would follow up his silly story.

Then Lloyd asked me if I remembered the diner where we had drunk coffee after the party, and the walk along the river early the following morning. I disagreed with him gently, and explained that our conversation had taken place on the balcony. I told him that I had gone to the guest room to look for my wrap and that he had been standing by the window looking down at the traffic. I didn't tell him that I had been exasperated by his bulky body that had forced me against the railings, nor that I had found his damp hand on my bare shoulder repulsive. I did tell him, however, that I had returned to my apartment alone.

Lloyd shook his head. He got up from his chair, straightened his jacket and started to walk towards the colonnade.

'You've got a real bad memory, Frances Daye,' he said turning to me and grinning. 'I think you're just making it up.'

Lloyd Harbin came to Paris for three springs, and each year he tried to get closer. I guess he was building up to something, but I didn't give him the chance to say it. After a while I slunk away from him, growling softly like a bad-tempered cat. I think he must have understood because he didn't visit again. In the winter of the third year he wrote to me saying that he had married a woman slightly older than himself.

I worked throughout that decade until the commissions grew thin. I was told then that there were others who wrote more convincingly and were able to devise recipes simple enough for the busy housewife, compromised by time and ingredients. I was upset by the rejections, more than I should have been. I let my hair go grey and my tan fade, and I forgot to buy lipstick. I retired to my apartment and shut the door. There seemed no reason to go out.

I stayed inside for a very long time, although how I filled the hours I do not remember because I had ceased to write. I think that, like Vivien, I must have paced around the sitting room, or taken down a book from the shelf and tried to read. Gradually, however, I realised that despite my reluctance to engage with the city, for the sake of my sanity I should try to leave the apartment for a short time every day. Slowly I learned to invent a little chore – a loaf of bread to buy, a trip to the dry cleaners. Over the years it has become a discipline to devise a daily task that takes me away from my rooms.

I have created a strict routine. Once I have fabricated my reason to go downstairs, I look out of the window to check on the weather. I put on my coat and gloves, and inspect my image in the mirror. I wait until any footsteps from the neighbouring apartments have faded away and then I open the door, lock it behind me and descend the stairs to the hallway. I speak to no one apart from Madame Espisito, the concierge, to whom I say, 'Bonjour.' Her *loge* is situated at the entrance. From there she observes who comes and goes, and she sorts the mail at her table before slipping it into the metal boxes that line one wall of the entrance.

One day in the winter of last year, I had just returned from my errand. I had bought a bottle of milk from the *crémerie*, and as I stepped into the hallway I noticed that the condensation on the glass bottle had dampened my gloves. I was inspecting the wet stains on the yellow leather when the concierge came out of her *loge* carrying a package for me. Although Madame Espisito wore flowered overalls and aprons that disguised her figure, she was startling, like Sophia Loren, dark-skinned and doe-eyed, with a round bun of black hair curled at the back of her head. She possessed a saint's face, I think, a face that radiated goodness. She came towards me that morning and handed me the package, saying it was too big for the mail box. The envelope was addressed correctly and postmarked Paris, but it was torn and creased. It looked as though it had fallen from a conveyor belt in the sorting office and lain forgotten for years, or had been stuffed into the wrong mail box which had only just been emptied. The envelope smelled musty and there was dust in the creases of the thick brown paper.

It surprises me now that I did not open the package straight away, the moment that I entered my apartment. Something must have prevented me from doing so: maybe the telephone rang, although it rings so rarely, or perhaps a window was banging in the bedroom or the bathroom. I put the envelope on top of the mail that I heap on a dining chair, and I pushed the chair back under the table, as I habitu-ally do, to hide the pile. It wasn't until the evening that I remembered the package again. Then, I opened it slowly without enthusiasm, for in my opinion brown envelopes always contain problems: rejections of stories or articles I have written, or documents from solicitors or bank managers that require immediate attention. I slid my finger under the flap and broke the seal, but when I looked inside I found only a thin buff coloured notebook.

There was no accompanying letter, no note or card. Nor was there a name on the front cover of the book, only a date, May 1960. The text began on the first page and was written in a hand that I did not recognise. Certain passages were in French, others in English, as if the writer had simply found it easier at certain moments to express herself in one or other language. The handwriting itself was scratchy and, in places, the ink had run out so that all I could see were the colourless marks left by the dry pen. I spent most of that night trying to distinguish the close slanting words one by one, until finally I found a magnifying glass to make out the shapes. I read until my eyes hurt, but I understood nothing.

The following day I translated the French passages. Then I copied out the notes in my own hand and when I reached the end I found that I had written four distinct texts. The first three were merely fragments, but the last was a complete story. I immediately thought of Ania. I suppose I hoped that she had sent them to me as some sort of recompense for disappearing, and that these notes were an attempt to communicate a veiled account of what had happened. I guessed that she had written them long ago and had forgotten to post them.

Reading the stories again that evening, I realised, however, that I was wrong. They weren't written by Ania after all. I doubted that she could have remembered these things or that she would have retold them in such a way. As I ran my eyes over the words for the third time, it began to dawn on me who the author was.

They were my mother's stories, I was sure of that. But I knew, as I looked down at the notebook and ran my fingers across the text, that she had not written them.

The stories were my own.

THE LAST STORY

What does the girl feel now?

She feels the soles of her shoes against the paving stones and the bite of her knife-edge nails cutting the skin inside her clenched fists.

What does the girl know?

That she walks in a circle, or a chain of circles, aimlessly round and round.

A woman opens a window and calls to the girl, asking her to stop and come inside. She looks down at the girl's shoes that are as cracked as old skin. She looks at the dress hanging like sadness from the girl's shoulders. She takes the hat that smells of basements and damp corners. Then she brings the girl a glass and pours her water from a jug, hands her a dish of apricots, and peels her an apple with a small knife that is diamond sharp.

Quietly, while the apple peel browns and twists in the fire, the woman asks the girl why she walks in circles.

'I can't escape.' she replies. 'I can't move forward to the future. I'm lost inside the past. It spirals round me, carries me with it. It makes me pace in circles. Time moves,' she says wearily, 'I see it move.' She points to the clock on the mantelpiece, 'but it is meaningless. Time is only the wound-up hands of a clock, mechanical. Time has no sense.'

'Tell me about your past,' says the woman. 'Tell me what you want for the future.'

Slowly the girl speaks. She talks about the pictures that she carries with

her: the house and the garden, the family, the mother and father, the child
standing on the pile of stones.

'I lost them,' she says. 'Better to move on, start again.'

The woman silently takes the girl by her arm. She leads her to another
room, a garden room with windows that open onto orange trees and palms.
Draped over a table are lengths of cloth that roll down to the floor, billowing
like coloured sails in the breeze. She pulls out a length of silk and stretches
it out over the table.

'I shall make you a dress,' she says.

The girl is grateful, but confused. She says nothing but dreamily touches
the cloth with her long-nailed fingers, feeling the peaks and troughs of the
weave as it runs over her skin.

The woman has rung for the maid. She whispers to her by the door.
Then she calls to the girl who is told that she must rest. She is taken upstairs
to an attic room where the walls are the shade of a moth's wing and the
floorboards are uncovered. Strangely, the bareness of the room eases her
for there are no distracting patterns and pictures here.

She sleeps for one night, maybe more. She cannot tell how long she
lies in the room but when she wakes it is daylight. Opening her eyes, she
remembers where she is. Now, beside the bed stands a chair of black and
gold lacquer, aged and handsome in the empty room, and lying across its
upholstered seat is a dress as grey as the walls. At first the girl is disappointed. She likes bright colours and had hoped the dress would be cut
from the gold or silver silk that she had seen in the garden room. She lies
for a while looking at the dead grey fabric, then she stretches out her hand
to touch it. It is not, after all, as she has imagined it, for as she touches
the cloth, it becomes silk, and the greyness is transformed into greens and
blues, each tone dissolving into the other like water-colour. Stitched over
the silk is a pattern of gold embroidered lines, abstract shapes that have no
meaning for her.

Because of its fineness, the dress has been lined with a heavier silk.
On this lining, which is the colour of skin, are tiny flesh-toned stitches,

chain stitch lines that are hidden right inside the dress. They are embroidered drawings of the things she had described to the woman the day before. The stitches are so small that when she slides her finger across the silk she cannot feel them. The discordance between the beauty of the embroidery and the sad, bitter images that it depicts shock her. She looks at each picture and remembers it, but when she pulls the dress over her head, when the pictures are pressed next to her skin, she forgets them immediately. All she can see is the silk chiffon that changes colour as she moves, and the shimmering gold of the thread that runs through the fabric.

She moves forward, down the stairs to the salon. Her pace is steady and direct. Her arms are relaxed and her hands unclenched. Her fingers touch the lightness of the dress.

In the salon the woman smiles at the girl. She invites her to sit at a small table where a breakfast of rolls, butter, thin spiced ham and coffee has been prepared. As the girl eats, relishing the flavours, the woman talks about the dress.

She says that it is made up of two parts, the future and the past, the shell and the lining. They are joined together by a seam that runs all around the dress from the neck to the hem.

'This is the present,' says the woman. 'The present is only a seam that attaches the future to the past because the future relentlessly becomes the past. The future is what you have asked for. The past is what you have lived and is hidden in the lining. You will forget it when you wear the dress.'

The girl, having finished her breakfast, is anxious to move on. She stands up and walks towards the hallway. Before she steps outside the door, however, the woman puts her hand gently upon the girl's shoulder.

'The dress will not last for ever,' she says. It will grow thin. The moths will make holes and weaken the thread. It will tear and wear away, and only the flesh-coloured stitches will remain. But then your hair will be white and your bones will ache. You won't care about the future. Then you *will remember the past again; it will be the right time. You will remember it like the pictures embroidered on the dress, like dreams.'*

But the girl doesn't hear. She has already begun to walk away, beyond the front door and out onto the street in a straight line.